The Nightingale that Shrieked and Other Tales

OTHER OXFORD BOOKS FOR CHILDREN BY
KEVIN CROSSLEY-HOLLAND

Beowulf

The Green Children

Why the Fish Laughed and Other Tales

Short! A Book of Very Short Stories

The Nightingale that Shrieked
and Other Tales

Edited by Kevin Crossley-Holland

OXFORD
UNIVERSITY PRESS

Great Clarendon Street, Oxford OX2 6DP

Oxford University Press is a department of the University of Oxford.
It furthers the University's objective of excellence in research, scholarship,
and education by publishing worldwide in

Oxford New York
Auckland Bangkok Buenos Aires Cape Town Chennai
Dar es Salaam Delhi Hong Kong Istanbul Karachi Kolkata
Kuala Lumpur Madrid Melbourne Mexico City Mumbai Nairobi
São Paulo Shanghai Singapore Taipei Tokyo Toronto

with an associated company in Berlin

Oxford is a registered trade mark of Oxford University Press
in the UK and in certain other countries

These stories first published in *The Young Oxford Book of Folk* Tales 1998
First published in this paperback edition 2002

British Library Cataloguing in Publication Data available

ISBN 0 19 275188 3

1 3 5 7 9 10 8 6 4 2

Printed in Great Britain by
Cox & Wyman Ltd, Reading, Berkshire

For Sally and Dick and their children and grandchildren

Contents

The Power of Love

A young man was intending to get married, when suddenly Death appeared and stood in front of him.

'You shall die on your wedding day,' he said.

Petrified with fear, the young man could not utter a single word. He wandered sadly off until he came to the foot of Mount Biledjan. He looked up and saw an old man with a white beard seated upon an aery throne, a staff in his hand. The old man's face shone with a bright light.

'Why are you so pale, boy?' asked the old man. 'Where are you going?'

'I'm running away from Death,' replied the young man. 'I'm in grave trouble, that's for sure!'

The old man smiled grimly, nodded his head and stroked his beard.

'Nobody has ever yet managed to escape from that mangy bag-o'-bones, sure enough!' he said. 'But I'll tell you something: his beard is firmly in *my* grasp, and *I* tell him when to take the soul of such and such a man, or shorten the life of such and such another, or lengthen that of such and such another.'

'Who are you then, grandfather?'

'They call me Time.'

'If you have such power, let me fall at your feet and beg you to save me! You can see that I'm still very young, and full of vigour. Why does he encompass my downfall? What have I done to him?'

The old man was moved.

'For so long as you remain terrified of Death, you will flee him, and remain for ever homeless,' he said. 'So walk one hundred paces to my right until you come to a wild plum tree. There you will find a well with water as limpid as the eye of a crane. Drink of that water, and the taste shall rid you of your fear, and the spirit of fortitude shall rise within you. Then go your way, and God be with you.'

The young man kissed the old man's hand, thanked him, found the well, drank the magic water which rid him of his fear and inspired him with fortitude, and went on his way. He marched on and on, until he came to a city built at the edge of a great sea. Here he settled for a few years, earned himself a small fortune, and then made his way back home to his mother and father. No sooner had he crossed the threshold, however, when, hey presto! there stood Death in front of him!

'So you thought you'd escape me, did you?' said Death. 'Who can extricate himself from my clutches, pray? It's all up with you now! Come on, hand over your soul!'

The young man's mother darted in between them.

'Why do you kill my young son?' she cried. 'If you must have someone's soul, take mine!'

Death started to tug at her soul, till it began to leave her feet and move up through her windpipe. The old woman could not stand it for long. 'Help, Death is ravishing my soul!' she cried.

Death relaxed his grip.

The young man's father darted forward.

'Do not kill my only son, the pillar and light of my house!' he cried. 'If you must have someone's soul, take mine!'

Death started to draw his soul till it left his legs and moved up past his tongue. The old man could not stand it for long.

'Help me, son! Death is robbing me of my soul to save your life!' he cried.

Death relaxed his grip.

'I cannot blame them,' said the young man. 'There is no need for them to suffer for my sake. But since you are here, let us go to the house of my betrothed. If she is not prepared to sacrifice up her soul for me, then most gladly will I surrender my own!'

So Death and the young man went to the house of his intended bride. As soon as the girl saw the young man, Death had no time to set to work before she ran up, threw her arms round the young man's neck, and kissed him warmly. So close was their embrace, it seemed they were but one body and soul.

'Ho there!' shouted Death. 'That's enough! I've no more time to waste. Tell me what you wish to do!'

'What do *you* want?' asked the girl.

'I am here to take your young man's soul!' said Death.

'If you must take someone's soul, take mine!' said the girl.

Death began to tug at her soul, till it slowly came away at the tips of her toes and the roots of her hair.

'Why are you torturing me so?' cried the girl. 'If you want my soul, take it at one go! Let me only first kiss my betrothed, as I yearn to do, and then do as you will!'

Death snatched away the girl's soul with one sharp tug. No sooner had he done so, however, than he began to marvel at her great love and devotion, and being unable to dismiss the young man and the young woman from his mind, he relented, and he gave her back her soul, and left them together, and went on his way.

The young man and his betrothed returned home in great joy. For three days and three nights the wedding festivities continued, and they achieved their hearts' desire.

Three apples fell from Heaven: one for the bride, one for the bridegroom, and one for the white-bearded old man, who was, is, and ever shall be, until the End of Time. Amen.

The Forty Thieves

In a town in Persia there dwelt two brothers, one named Cassim, the other Ali Baba. Cassim was married to a rich wife and lived in plenty, while Ali Baba had to maintain his wife and children by cutting wood in a neighbouring forest and selling it in the town. One day, when Ali Baba was in the forest, he saw a troop of men on horseback, coming towards him. He was afraid they were robbers, and climbed into a tree for safety. When they came up to him and dismounted, he counted forty of them.

The finest man among them, whom Ali Baba took to be their captain, went a little way among some bushes, and said, 'Open, Sesame!' so plainly that Ali Baba heard him. A door opened in the rocks, and having made the troop go in, he followed them, and the door shut again of itself. Ali Baba, fearing they might come out and catch him, was forced to sit patiently in the tree. At last the door opened again, and the Forty Thieves came out.

The captain then closed the door, saying, 'Shut, Sesame!' Every man mounted, the captain put himself at their head, and they returned as they came.

Then Ali Baba climbed down and went to the door concealed among the bushes, and said, 'Open, Sesame!' and it flew open. Ali Baba, who expected a dull, dismal place, was greatly surprised to find it large and well lighted. He saw rich bales of merchandise—silk, stuff-brocades all piled together, and gold and silver in heaps, and money in leather purses.

He went in and the door shut behind him. He did not look at the silver, but brought out as many bags of gold as he thought his asses could carry, loaded them with the bags, and hid it all with faggots. Using the words, 'Shut, Sesame!' he closed the door and went home.

Then he drove his asses into the yard, carried the money bags to his wife, and emptied them out before her. He bade her keep the secret, and he would go and bury the gold.

'Let me first measure it,' said his wife. 'I will go and borrow a measure from someone, while you dig the hole.' So she ran to the wife of Cassim and borrowed a measure. Knowing Ali Baba's poverty, the sister was curious to find out what sort of grain his wife wished to measure, and artfully put some suet at the bottom of the measure.

Ali Baba's wife went home and set the measure on the heap of gold, and filled it and emptied it often, to her great content. She then carried it back to her sister, without noticing that a piece of gold was sticking to it, which Cassim's wife perceived directly her back was turned.

She grew very curious, and said to Cassim, 'Cassim, your brother is richer than you. He does not count his money, he measures it.' He begged her to explain this riddle, which she did by showing him the piece of money and telling him where she found it.

Cassim grew envious and went to his brother in the morning before sunrise. 'Ali Baba,' he said, showing him the gold piece, 'you pretend to be poor and yet you measure gold.'

By this Ali Baba perceived that through his wife's folly Cassim and his wife knew their secret, so he confessed all and offered Cassim a share.

'That I expect,' said Cassim, 'but I must know where to find the treasure, otherwise I will discover all, and you will lose all.' Ali Baba, more out of kindness than fear, told him of the cave, and the very words to use.

Cassim left Ali Baba, meaning to get the treasure for himself. He rose early next morning, and set out with ten mules loaded with great chests. He soon found the place, and the door in the rock.

He said, 'Open, Sesame!' and the door opened and shut behind him.

He hastened to gather together as much of the treasure as possible, but when he was ready to go he could not remember what to say for thinking of his great riches. Instead of 'Sesame,' he said, 'Open, Barley!' and the door remained fast. He named several different sorts of grain, all but the right one, and the door still stuck fast. He was so frightened at the danger he was in that he had as much forgotten the word as if he had never heard it.

About noon the robbers returned to their cave, and saw Cassim's mules roving about with great chests on their backs. This gave them the alarm: they drew their sabres, and went to the door, which opened on their captain's saying: 'Open, Sesame!'

Cassim, who had heard the trampling of their horses' feet, resolved to sell his life dearly, so when the door opened he leaped out and threw the captain down. In vain, however, for the robbers with their sabres soon killed him. On entering the cave they saw all the bags laid ready, and could not imagine how anyone had got in without knowing their secret. They cut Cassim's body into four quarters, and nailed them up inside the cave, in order to frighten anyone who should venture in, and went away in search of more treasure.

As night drew on Cassim's wife grew very uneasy, and ran to her brother-in-law, and told him where her husband had gone. Ali Baba did his best to comfort her, and set out to the forest in search of Cassim. The first thing he saw on entering the cave was his dead brother. Full of horror, he put the body on one of his asses, and bags of gold on the other two, and, covering all with some faggots, returned home. He drove the two asses laden with gold into his own yard, and led the other to Cassim's house. The door was opened by the slave Morgiana, whom he knew to be both brave and cunning.

Unloading the ass, he said to her, 'This is the body of your master, who has been murdered, but whom we must bury as though he had died in his bed. I will speak with you again, but now tell your mistress I am come.'

The wife of Cassim, on learning the fate of her husband, broke out into cries and tears, but Ali Baba offered to take her to live with him and his wife if she would promise to keep his counsel and leave everything to Morgiana; whereupon she agreed, and dried her eyes.

Morgiana, meanwhile, sought an apothecary and asked him for some lozenges. 'My poor master,' she said, 'can neither eat nor speak, and no one knows what his distemper is.' She carried home the lozenges and returned next day weeping, and asked for an essence only given to those just about to die. Thus, in the evening, no one was surprised to hear the wretched shrieks and cries of Cassim's wife and Morgiana, telling everyone that Cassim was dead.

The day after Morgiana went to an old cobbler near the gates of the town, put a piece of gold in his hand, and bade him follow her with his needle and thread. Having bound his eyes with a handkerchief, she took him to the room where the body lay, pulled off the bandage, and bade him sew the quarters together, after which she covered his eyes again and led him home. Then they buried Cassim, and Morgiana his slave followed him to the grave, weeping and tearing her hair, while Cassim's wife stayed at home uttering lamentable cries. Next day she went to live with Ali Baba, who gave Cassim's shop to his eldest son.

The Forty Thieves, on their return to the cave, were much astonished to find Cassim's body gone and some of their money bags. 'We are certainly discovered,' said the captain, 'and shall be undone if we cannot find out who it is that knows our secret. Two men must have known it; we have killed one, we must now find the other. To this end one of you must go into the city and discover whom we have killed, and whether men talk of the strange manner of his death. If the messenger fails he must lose his life, lest we be betrayed.'

One of the thieves offered to do this, disguised himself, and happened to enter the town at daybreak, just by Baba Mustapha's stall. The thief bade him good day, saying, 'Honest man, how can you possibly see to stitch at your age?'

'Old as I am,' replied the cobbler, 'I have very good eyes, and you will believe me when I tell you that I sewed a dead body together in a place where I had less light than I have now.'

The robber was overjoyed at his good fortune, and, giving him a piece of gold, desired to be shown the house where he stitched up the dead body.

At first Mustapha refused, saying that he had been blindfolded; but when the robber gave him another piece of gold he began to think he might remember the turnings if blindfolded as before. This plan succeeded; the robber partly led him, and was partly guided by him, right in front of Cassim's house, the door of which the robber marked with a piece of chalk. Then, well pleased, he bade farewell to Baba Mustapha and returned to the forest.

By-and-by Morgiana, going out, saw the mark the robber had made, quickly guessed that some mischief was brewing, and fetching a piece of chalk marked two or three doors on each side, without saying anything to her master or mistress.

The thief, meantime, told his comrades of his discovery. The captain thanked him, and bade him show him the house he had marked. But when they came to it they saw that five or six of the houses were chalked in the same manner. The guide was at once beheaded for having failed. Another robber was despatched, and, having won over Baba Mustapha, marked the house in red chalk;

but Morgiana being again too clever for them, the second messenger was put to death also.

The captain now resolved to go himself, but, wiser than the others, he did not mark the house, but looked at it so closely that he could not fail to remember it. He ordered his men to go into the neighbouring villages and buy nineteen mules, and thirty-eight leather jars, all empty, except one which was full of oil. The captain put one of his men, fully armed, into each, rubbing the outside of the jars with oil from the full vessel. Then the nineteen mules were loaded with thirty-seven robbers in jars, and the jar of oil, and reached the town by dusk.

The captain stopped his mules in front of Ali Baba's house, and said to Ali Baba, who was sitting outside for coolness, 'I have brought some oil from a distance to sell at tomorrow's market, but it is now so late that I know not where to pass the night, unless you will take me in.'

Though Ali Baba had seen the captain of the robbers in the forest, he did not recognize him in the disguise of an oil merchant. He bade him welcome and went to Morgiana to bid her prepare a bed and supper for his guest. After they had supped he went again to speak to Morgiana in the kitchen, while the captain went into the yard to tell his men what to do.

Beginning at the first jar he said to each man, 'As soon as I throw some stones from the window of the chamber where I lie, cut the jars open with your knives and come out and I will be with you in a trice.' He returned to the house, and Morgiana led him to his chamber.

She then told Abdallah, her fellow-slave, to set on the pot to make some broth for her master, who had gone to bed. Meanwhile her lamp went out, and she had no more oil in the house.

'Do not be uneasy,' said Abdallah, 'go into the yard and take some out of one of those jars.'

Morgiana took the oil pot, and went into the yard. When she came to the first jar the robber inside said softly, 'Is it time?'

Any other slave but Morgiana, on finding a man in the jar instead of the oil she wanted, would have screamed and made a noise; but she, knowing the danger her master was in, bethought herself of a plan, and answered quietly, 'Not yet, but presently.' She went to all the jars, giving the same answer, till she came to the jar of oil. She now saw that her master, thinking to entertain an oil merchant, had let thirty-eight robbers into his house.

She filled her oil pot, went back to the kitchen and, having lit her lamp, went again to the oil jar and filled a large kettle full of oil. When it boiled she went and poured enough oil into every jar to stifle and kill the robber inside. When this brave deed was done she went back to the kitchen and waited to see what would happen.

In a quarter of an hour the captain of the robbers awoke, got up, and opened the window. As all seemed quiet he threw down some little pebbles which hit the jars. He listened, and as none of his men seemed to stir he grew uneasy, and went down into the yard. On going to the first jar and saying, 'Are you asleep?' he smelt the hot boiled oil, and knew at once that his plot to murder Ali Baba and his household had been discovered.

He found all the gang were dead, and, missing the oil out of the last jar, became aware of the manner of their death. He then forced the lock of a door leading into a garden and made his escape. Morgiana heard and saw all this, and, rejoicing at her success, went to bed and fell asleep.

At daybreak Ali Baba arose, and, seeing the oil jars there still, asked why the merchant had not gone with his mules. Morgiana bade him look in the first jar and see if there was any oil. Seeing a man, he started back in terror. 'Have no fear,' said Morgiana, 'the man cannot harm you: he is dead.'

Ali Baba, when he had recovered somewhat from his astonishment, asked what had become of the merchant. 'Merchant!' said she. 'He is no more a merchant than I am!' And she told him the whole story, assuring him that it was a plot of the robbers of whom only three were left, and that the white and red chalk marks had something to do with it. Ali Baba at once gave Morgiana her freedom, saying that he owed her his life. They then buried the bodies in Ali Baba's garden, while the mules were sold in the market.

The captain returned to his lonely cave and firmly resolved to avenge his companions by killing Ali Baba. He dressed himself carefully, and went into the town, where he took lodgings in an inn. In the course of a great many journeys to the forest he carried away many rich stuffs and much fine linen, and set up a shop opposite that of Ali Baba's son. He called himself Cogia Hassan, and as he was both civil and well dressed he soon made friends with Ali Baba's son, and through him with Ali Baba, whom he was continually asking to sup with him.

Ali Baba, wishing to return his kindness, invited him into his house, thanking him for his kindness to his son. When the merchant was about to take his leave Ali Baba stopped him, saying, 'Where are you going, sir, in such haste? Will you not stay and sup with me?'

The merchant refused, saying that he had a reason; and, on Ali Baba's asking him what that was, he replied, 'It is, sir, that I can eat no victuals that have any salt in them.'

'If that is all,' said Ali Baba, 'let me tell you that there shall be no salt in either the meat or the bread that we eat tonight.'

He went to give this order to Morgiana, who was much surprised. 'Who is this man,' she said, 'who eats no salt with his meat?'

'He is an honest man, Morgiana,' returned her master, 'therefore do as I bid you.'

But she desired to see this strange man, so she helped Abdallah to carry up the dishes, and saw in a moment that Cogia Hassan was the robber captain and carried a dagger under his garment. 'I am not surprised,' she said to herself, 'that this wicked man, who intends to kill my master, will eat no salt with him; but I will hinder his plans.'

She sent up the supper by Abdallah, while she made ready. When the dessert had been served, Cogia Hassan was left alone with Ali Baba and his son, whom he thought to make drunk and then to murder them. Morgiana, meanwhile, put on a head-dress like a dancing-girl's, and clasped a girdle round her waist, from which hung a dagger with a silver hilt, and said to Abdallah, 'Take your tabor, and let us go and divert our master and his guest.'

Abdallah took his tabor and played before Morgiana until they came to the door, where Abdallah stopped playing and Morgiana made a low curtsy. 'Come in, Morgiana,' said Ali Baba, 'and let Cogia Hassan see what you can do.' Turning to Cogia Hassan, he said, 'She's my slave and my housekeeper.'

Cogia Hassan was by no means pleased, for he feared that his chance of killing Ali Baba was gone for the present; but he pretended great eagerness to see Morgiana. After she had performed several dances she drew her dagger and made passes with it, as if it were part of the dance. Suddenly, out of breath, she snatched the tabor from Abdallah with her left hand, and, holding the dagger in her right, held out the tabor to her master. Ali Baba and his son put a piece of gold into it, and Cogia Hassan, seeing that she was coming to him, pulled out his purse to make her a present, but while he was putting his hand into it Morgiana plunged the dagger into his heart.

'Unhappy girl!' cried Ali Baba and his son. 'What have you done to ruin us?'

'It was to preserve you, master, not to ruin you,' answered Morgiana. 'See here,' opening the false merchant's garment and showing the dagger. 'See what an enemy you have entertained! Remember, he would eat no salt with you, and what more would you have? Look at him! He is both the false oil merchant and the captain of the Forty Thieves.'

Ali Baba was so grateful to Morgiana for thus saving his life that he offered her to his son in marriage, who readily consented, and a few days after the wedding was celebrated with great splendour.

At the end of a year Ali Baba, hearing nothing of the two remaining robbers, judged they were dead, and set out to the cave. The door opened on his saying, 'Open, Sesame!' He went in, and saw that nobody had been there since the captain left it. He brought away as much gold as he could carry, and returned to town. He told his son the secret of the cave, which his son handed down in his turn, so the children and grandchildren of Ali Baba were rich to the end of their lives.

Trousers Mehmet and the Sultan's Daughter

Once there was and twice there wasn't a clever village boy named Mehmet. When his old father died, leaving him nothing but a pair of baggy trousers and his blessing, Mehmet stored the blessing in his heart. Then, putting the trousers over his shoulder, he set one foot before the other till he came to Istanbul.

No work, no bread, thought he. Though I can read, I've learned no trade, so I shall carry burdens to earn my keep. And since I have neither basket nor rope, these trousers must serve as my sack.

A kind old tailor sewed the trouser legs shut. Then, 'Hamal! Porter!' he shouted. 'Let Trousers Mehmet carry your bundles!'

'Trousers Mehmet, here's a package!' Soon Mehmet's cheerful face appeared in shops and markets throughout the city, and he had work a-plenty.

One day just as he left Sirkeci Station carrying a heavy load, he saw a splendid procession on its way from Topkapi Palace to the Covered Bazaar. In a golden litter sat the sultan's daughter, with her merry brown eyes smiling at him above her veil.

'Ah, how I could love that lady!' sighed Mehmet as he watched.

'But she's far too fine to love a poor hamal like me.'

As for the princess, the handsome hamal had touched her heart. 'There is a young man who truly pleases me,' she murmured. 'But what can bring a princess and a porter together?'

Amid the bustle and the chatter of the Covered Bazaar, the princess thought long and longer about Trousers Mehmet. Suddenly she had an idea.

The next morning, she went before the sultan. 'Father, is it not time for me to be married?' she asked.

'Married!' he exclaimed. 'For two years, young men have come seeking your hand. But would you choose one? Not at all!'

'Father, none of them was half as clever as you,' she said, 'and therefore none of them would do.'

'And how am I to find such a clever young man?' asked the sultan, pleased by his daughter's compliment.

'You could set a task so difficult that only the cleverest of men could complete it,' she suggested.

The sultan considered the matter. Then, 'Yes, my daughter,' he decided. 'I shall send envoys to every kingdom inviting princes to compete for my daughter's hand.'

'Only princes, father?' she asked. 'It is not only princes who are clever.'

'You are right, my daughter,' he agreed.

And, true enough, criers were sent out immediately shouting, 'Come! Come! Whoever seeks to wed the princess must come to Topkapi Palace!'

Within three or five days, young men of every shape and size and station had gathered at the palace. Even Trousers Mehmet joined the throng. He loved the princess already, and no one had said that hamals could not try for her hand.

Looking directly at the suitors, the sultan himself announced, 'The man who wins my daughter must bring to me one who hunts, who throws away what he catches, and who carries with him what he cannot find.'

The suitors stared at one another. Who could make sense of such a task as that? Clearly, the sultan had lost his wits. One by one, they turned away, except for Trousers Mehmet. He stood there, thinking. The sultan was said to be a clever man. Perhaps this was a riddle . . . not one to be found in books, but on the lips of the people.

As Mehmet went out slowly into the busy street, the muezzin called from a minaret of Sultan Ahmet mosque. 'It is time for noonday prayer,' said Mehmet. 'After that, I shall think about the sultan's task.'

He hurried to Ablutions Fountain in the mosque yard. There he washed himself three times. Then, leaving his shoes at the mosque door, he went inside to pray.

As Mehmet passed a public fountain after the holy service, he saw a wretched peasant making himself clean. His washing done, the peasant set about that unpleasant bit of business known to the poor the world over.

Mehmet smiled. Then suddenly his heart pounded, tum tum tum. Was this by any chance the kind of hunter the sultan meant? He went to the peasant. 'Brother,' he said, 'if you will come with me for half an hour, I shall buy your bread and cheese for three or five days.'

The peasant stared at Mehmet. 'Empty words do not fill an empty stomach,' he grumbled. Then, as Mehmet still stood there, he said, 'First I must finish what I am doing, son. Then I shall come.'

'If you wish the bread and cheese, you must come now,' said Mehmet. 'You may finish what you are doing when we reach Topkapi Palace.'

'The sultan's palace!' exclaimed the peasant. 'Indeed not! My life is worth more to me than bread and cheese. Still, my father used to say that it's better to die on a full stomach than to live on an empty one . . .'

'Fear not,' said Mehmet. 'Only trust me, and you will see. Come.' And he and the peasant went directly to the palace.

Immediately, they were taken to the sultan. The ruler stared at Mehmet curiously. A hamal . . . with an old pair of trousers for a basket! And he had a ragged peasant with him, itching and scratching. 'Well,' said the sultan, 'what is your business here?'

'This morning, sire,' said Mehmet, 'you set a task for the man who wished to wed your daughter. I have brought the hunter you described.' Then, turning to the peasant, Mehmet said, 'Now, brother, you may finish that business you began at the fountain.'

Obediently, the peasant began to search among his tattered clothes for lice. As he found a louse, he would flatten it on his thumbnail and then throw it away. One, two, three, four, five—and still he scratched.

'Enough!' said the sultan, smiling a little despite himself.

'Well, sire,' asked Mehmet, 'have I not brought to you one who hunts, who throws away what he catches, and who carries with him what he cannot find?'

'You have,' agreed the sultan.

'Praise be to Allah!' said Mehmet happily. And from his worn purse, he gave the peasant a handful of coins. 'Eat with a hearty appetite, brother,' he said, 'and thank you. May your way be open.' The peasant left, pleased with this strange bargain.

'Now,' said Mehmet eagerly, 'when may I marry your daughter?'

The sultan's eyes glittered coldly. 'Not so fast,' he warned. 'I do not intend to have my daughter marry a hamal.'

'But, sire,' Mehmet said, 'you promised . . .'

'I know,' interrupted the sultan angrily. 'But how could I guess that a porter would seek her hand? Naturally, a hamal would be well acquainted with lice! No, you cannot have my daughter, unless . . . unless you succeed in a second task, and then a third. Then you may have my daughter.'

Mehmet swallowed his anger and disappointment. 'Very well, sire,' he said. 'What is the second task?'

The sultan thought for a moment. Then he replied, 'You must

bring me life which enters an empty box alone, yet comes out bringing death with it.'

Mehmet's shoulders sagged, but he bowed and left the sultan's presence. 'Fair or unfair, he is none the less the sultan,' the hamal murmured, 'and the father of the lovely princess. Thorns and roses surely grow on the same tree! Still, Allah willing, I shall win the sultan's daughter.'

He straightened his shoulders and went directly to the Covered Bazaar. 'At least,' he decided, 'I can buy a box while I am thinking.'

He searched among the stalls until he found a small wooden box with a snug cover. Paying the shopkeeper, he tucked the box into his sash.

As he was leaving the Bazaar, he heard the boom-boom-boom of a drum and the mellow piping of a zurna. 'Come and see!' a showman sang, and the crowd hurried to his stall. 'Wonders from India.' 'Wonders from China.' 'See something you have never seen before—a miracle!' Mehmet read the bold signs above the stall.

For a moment forgetting his own problem, Mehmet smiled. 'Man is truly as old as his head, not his years. Just see the crowd scramble!'

Suddenly he noticed something special. 'From Egypt,' the sign said. As he reached out to touch what he saw, the showman shouted, 'Take your hands off that cage. There's trouble inside.'

'I'll pay you well for just half of that trouble,' said Mehmet quietly, and reached into his sash for his box and his purse.

'Do you know what you are buying?' asked the showman.

'I know what I am buying,' answered Mehmet. Carefully, carefully . . . in a moment, Mehmet had a small something in his box. And the showman had a large sum in his purse.

With his joy shortening his journey, Mehmet was soon at the palace. 'Well,' asked the sultan, 'have you brought life in a box?'

'Yes, sire, and it brings death with it when it leaves the box,' replied Trousers Mehmet. 'Here it is.'

The sultan turned the box over and over. Then he laughed. 'You are bold, young man, but how can you prove what you say? There is no way of seeing into that box of yours. Open it.'

'As you say, sire,' said Mehmet politely, and he lifted the cover just enough so that the sultan could see the gleaming eyes of a deadly asp.

'Shut it!' the sultan cried. And Mehmet shut the box.

'Well, sire,' said Mehmet, smiling, 'I have accomplished the second task. What is the third task to be?'

The sultan stared at the young hamal. Then slowly he drew forth his own silken handkerchief. Holding it out to Mehmet, he said, 'Bring me a thousand forests in this handkerchief.'

Mehmet took the handkerchief and slipped it safely into his sash. He studied the sultan's face, but it gave no hint of the answer. Had he come within a hair of winning his princess only to lose her on this puzzling task? Still, he kept the small bird of hope alive within his breast.

'This may be another riddle,' he mused as he left the palace and walked along the winding streets and through the main gate into Gülhane Park. As he wandered along a shady path, he murmured, 'I begin with the name of Allah. A thousand forests . . .' Suddenly there was a snapping sound beneath his foot. He moved his shoe, and—Allah be praised!—there lay an answer to the puzzle.

He picked up another just like the one he had crushed. Rolling the treasure inside the sultan's handkerchief, he tucked it gently into his sash. Then he hurried back to the palace.

'Well,' said the ruler, 'have you hidden the forests somewhere? I cannot see even the handkerchief.'

'Here, sire,' answered Trousers Mehmet, drawing it carefully from his sash. The sultan stared curiously as Mehmet unrolled the handkerchief and took out a single acorn.

A broad smile spread across the sultan's face. Who could deny that Allah proposed a thousand forests from that one acorn? And, indeed, who could doubt that Allah proposed this clever young man as a husband fit for the sultan's daughter?

Thus it was that Trousers Mehmet came to marry the sultan's daughter, in a wedding that lasted forty days and forty nights. May we all have a share in their happiness!

The Nightingale that Shrieked

This happened, or maybe it did not.
The time is long past, and much is forgot.

A king once sent his crier through the kingdom to inform the people that for three successive nights they must light neither lamp nor fire—that their houses must show no spark or glimmer of light or they would suffer terrible punishment. Then the king said to his minister, 'Now we shall judge for ourselves who obeys the sultan's word and who is careless of his command.'

Night fell, and the king and his minister disguised themselves to look like two wandering dervishes. Together they roamed the streets of the city, from which every straying foot had withdrawn, since the night was black as blindness. There was not a light to be seen. But on turning a corner, the two noticed a faint glow coming from a hut that stood by itself. They peeped through the window and saw three girls busily spinning wool in the light of a lamp which they had dimmed with an upturned sieve.

One girl was saying to the others, 'How I wish I were married to the sultan's baker! Then I should have bread to eat as often as I wanted.'

Another said, 'If only I were the wife of the sultan's cook! Then I should dine off meat every day of my life.'

But the youngest said, 'I would never consent to marry any lesser man than the sultan himself. If he made me his queen, within the year I should bear him twins—a boy with locks of silver and gold, and a girl for whom the sun shines when she smiles and the rain falls when she weeps.'

In the morning a messenger came from the palace to summon the three girls to the king's presence. The first two sisters sank on the doorstone and trembled, saying, 'Allah protect us as we stand between two fires. If we obey the king's command and do not work at night we die of hunger, and if we disobey we die of punishment.'

But the youngest sister told the messenger, 'Let the king send us fine robes to wear, for we are poor and have no clothes in which to enter a royal court.' And when the three girls stood before the king they wore gowns of velvet striped red and black.

They say, 'the talk of the evening is covered with butter and melts in the morning,' but the king married the eldest girl to his baker as she had wished and the next to his cook. The youngest girl who had said, 'I shall bear the sultan twins before the year is out, a boy with locks of silver and gold, and a girl for whom the sun shines when she smiles and the rain falls when she cries'—this girl he kept for himself. As soon as the necessary preparations were made, he married her according to the tradition of the prophet.

Who grew jealous of her? The king's old wife. As one before our time has said, 'When have women loved a fair-skinned girl or men loved a hero?' What did the old queen do? For a long time she did nothing, biding her time. She saw the new queen's belly rising, and she waited. She heard the midwife sitting at the new queen's pillow, chanting:

O great father Noah,
Who saved our souls,
Save this child in her hour of woe!

and she waited. But when the new queen gave birth to a pair of twins—as golden and as radiant as she had promised—the old queen said to the midwife, 'Take the newborn infants from their mother's side, and in their place put this little dog and this clay jar.'

Does not gold achieve all things? The midwife did the old queen's bidding and threw the two princelings into the palace garden.

Now the women began to wail and beat their cheeks. 'A calamity and a scandal! The king's new queen has given birth to a puppy dog and a water jug!' The king, ashamed, sent his queen away to live the life of a discarded wife.

What of the twins? Our God is praiseworthy indeed, for they were found by the king's gardener, whose wife was barren and had grown old childless. She pressed the babies to her breast, resting one on her right shoulder and one on her left, and nurtured them as if they had been the fruit of her own body.

The child in a tale grows fast. So it was with these two. In time the gardener built them a little house to live in. The fair brother with the locks of silver and gold, and his sister for whose smile the sun shone and for whose tears the rain fell, were such as fill the eye and set the tongue wagging. News of them reached the old queen, and once again she sent for the midwife to instruct her what to do.

The midwife waited until the brother had gone hunting and the girl was sitting in the house by herself. Then she knocked at the door and paid a visit. 'How perfect is this house!' she said. 'You lack nothing but the Tree of Apples that Dance and Apricots that Sing growing before your door. Then it would be complete.'

When the brother returned, he found his sister weeping. 'Why such tears?' he asked. And she told him of the midwife's visit, confessing that now she could not be truly happy until she had the magic fruit tree growing by her door. 'Gather up provisions for a journey; I shall set out tomorrow morning in search of your tree,' said her brother.

Next day the boy began to walk, trusting his fate to the All-Merciful. From place to place he travelled asking where he should seek the magic tree, but none knew how to advise him. At last he reached the foot of a high mountain. He climbed to its top, and there stood a Ghoul with one foot pointing to the east and one foot pointing to the west. The hair of his head was matted and covered his brow. The hair of his brow was thick and covered his eyes. 'Peace, O father Ghoul,' said the boy.

Had not your greeting
Preceded your speaking,
I should have torn you limb from limb
And snapped your bones and picked them clean!

the monster replied.

The boy went up to the Ghoul and cut the knotted hair on his head and shaved the bushy hair of his brows. The monster sighed with pleasure and said, 'You have brought back the light into my face, so may Allah light up your path before you. Tell me: what are you seeking and what have you come for?' The boy explained his search, and the Ghoul said, 'If you follow this road you will come to the land of Ghouls. The tree that you seek grows in the garden of the king. Its leaves are so broad that you could swaddle two infants in each. But first go to my brother. He is older than I am by one day and wiser by one year. Ask him to help you.'

The boy journeyed onward until ahead he saw the Ghoul's brother sitting in the middle of the path with his legs stretched out before him. 'Peace, O father Ghoul,' said the boy, and the monster replied as his brother had done,

Had not your greeting
Preceded your speaking,
I should have torn you limb from limb
And snapped your bones and picked them clean!

The boy did as he had done with the first Ghoul, snipping the hair that covered his forehead and trimming his eyebrows. Then the Ghoul asked, 'What has brought you from the land of men to the land of spirits and Djinn?'

'Allah brought me and I came,' the boy said. And he told the

Ghoul how he was looking for the Tree of Apples that Dance and Apricots that Sing to give to his sister.

The Ghoul said, 'Continue along this road, and you will see my sister sitting at her handmill grinding salt or fine white sugar. If you find her grinding salt, stop where you stand and do not let her see you. But if she should be grinding sugar, run to her as quickly as you can and nurse at each of her breasts. For once you have tasted her milk, she will do you no harm but help you as a mother helps her son.'

The boy did as the Ghoul had told him. Finding the Ghoul's sister milling sugar, he pounced on her right breast before she could look up and see who was coming. She said,

Whoever suckles the breast on my right
Is dear to my heart and a son in my sight.

When he turned to the other breast, she said,

Whoever suckles the breast on my left
Is dear as the son whom I love the best.

'What is the cause of your coming?' she asked the boy, 'and for what reason will you be going?' When he had told her about the Tree of Apples that Dance and Apricots that Sing, she said, 'Wait till my seven sons come home in the evening; they will help you. But for your protection I must hide you.' And she turned him into an onion like the other onions in her basket.

When it was dark the seven young Ghouls came home, saying, 'Mother, mother, there is about you a smell of men!'

She said, 'How can that be, when I have been sitting in this place all day long. It is you who have gone abroad and mingled with the humans in their towns, and their smell has clung to the tails of your gowns.'

Despite her words, the young Ghouls said, 'If you are hiding a woman we shall guard her like a sister, and if you are hiding a man we shall help him like a brother. May God protect him and visit a traitor's punishment on his betrayer.'

At that, their mother returned the boy to his own shape and

told her sons how he was searching for the Tree of Apples that Dance and Apricots that Sing. 'I know the place, and I can take him there in a month,' said the oldest son.

'I can lead him to it in a week,' said another.

And the youngest said, 'Climb on to my back, and I shall carry you there in the twinkling of an eye.'

So the boy flew on the youngest Ghoul's back to the garden of the king of Ghouls. With a monster's strength the young spirit uprooted the Tree of Apples that Dance and Apricots that Sing. And the boy took it to his sister to plant by the door of their house.

What did the king's old wife say when she saw that the boy with the locks of silver and gold had returned from his journey, whole and unharmed? She sent the midwife to visit his sister again. 'How cool it is in the shade of your tree, and how merry to see the apples dancing and hear the apricots sing!' the midwife said. 'Now indeed you own everything there is to own . . . except Bulbul Assiah, the Nightingale who Shrieks.'

'How can I find Bulbul Assiah?' the girl asked.

'He who brought you the tree of the dancing apples and singing apricots will surely bring you Bulbul Assiah,' the old woman said.

The sister told her brother about the nightingale and admitted that she could not live happily until she possessed it. The boy loved his sister, and to make her content, he set out once more. This time he took the shortest road to the home of the Ghouls, his adopted brothers. And the youngest flew with him to the aviary of the king of the Ghouls and showed him the cage that held Bulbul Assiah. The boy lifted it from its hook and brought it home to his sister.

Now the gardener, seeing the wonders that his children had collected—the tree with the dancing and singing fruits and the golden cage of Bulbul Assiah—went to the king and said, 'For forty years I have worked in your garden, yet you have never visited my house. Now I wish you to come and eat my food.'

'If Allah wills it, I shall come tomorrow,' said the king. Next day when the king entered the gardener's yard, the apples danced and the apricots sang on the tree in front of his children's house. And Bulbul Assiah began to shriek from his perch.

Who but a she-dog
Born of a she-dog
Knows how to whelp pups?
A queen can only bear
Noble lords and ladies fair.
Our sultan's wife bore no pup or jug of water
But a golden son and a comely daughter.
A boy with shining locks of gold and silver
A girl—why, the sun shines at her laughter.

So the king discovered that the brother and sister were his own twin son and daughter. He called their mother back from her seclusion and ordered a feast to last forty days and forty nights to celebrate her return.

As for the wicked old midwife,
May torments hound her all her life!

Zlateh the Goat

At Hanukkah time the road from the village to the town is usually covered with snow, but this year the winter had been a mild one. Hanukkah had almost come, yet little snow had fallen. The sun shone most of the time. The peasants complained that because of the dry weather there would be a poor harvest of winter grain. New grass sprouted, and the peasants sent their cattle out to pasture.

For Reuven the furrier it was a bad year, and after long hesitation he decided to sell Zlateh the goat. She was old and gave little milk. Feyvel the town butcher had offered eight gulden for her. Such a sum would buy Hanukkah candles, potatoes and oil for pancakes, gifts for the children, and other holiday necessaries for the house. Reuven told his oldest boy Aaron to take the goat to town.

Aaron understood what taking the goat to Feyvel meant, but he had to obey his father. Leah, his mother, wiped the tears from her eyes when she heard the news. Aaron's younger sisters, Anna and Miriam, cried loudly.

Aaron put on his quilted jacket and a cap with earmuffs, bound a rope around Zlateh's neck, and took along two slices of bread with cheese to eat on the road. Aaron was supposed to deliver the goat by evening, spend the night at the butcher's, and return the next day with the money.

While the family said goodbye to the goat, and Aaron placed the rope around her neck, Zlateh stood as patiently and good-naturedly as ever. She licked Reuven's hand. She shook her small white beard. Zlateh trusted human beings. She knew that they always fed her and never did her any harm.

When Aaron brought her out on the road to town, she seemed somewhat astonished. She'd never been led in that direction before. She looked back at him questioningly, as if to say, 'Where are you taking me?' But after a while she seemed to come to the conclusion that a goat shouldn't ask questions. Still, the road was different. They passed new fields, pastures, and huts with thatched roofs. Here and there a dog barked and came running after them, but Aaron chased it away with his stick.

The sun was shining when Aaron left the village. Suddenly the weather changed. A large black cloud with a bluish centre appeared in the east and spread itself rapidly over the sky. A cold wind blew in with it. The crows flew low, croaking. At first it looked as if it would rain, but instead it began to hail as in summer. It was early in the day, but it became dark as dusk. After a while the hail turned to snow.

In his twelve years Aaron had seen all kinds of weather, but he had never experienced a snow like this one. It was so dense it shut out the light of the day. In a short time their path was completely covered. The wind became as cold as ice. The road to town was narrow and winding. Aaron no longer knew where he was. He could not see through the snow. The cold soon penetrated his quilted jacket.

At first Zlateh didn't seem to mind the change in weather. She too was twelve years old and knew what winter meant. But when her legs sank deeper and deeper into the snow, she began to turn her head and look at Aaron in wonderment. Her mild eyes seemed to ask, 'Why are we out in such a storm?' Aaron hoped that a peasant would come along with his cart, but no one passed by.

The snow grew thicker, falling to the ground in large, whirling flakes. Beneath it Aaron's boots touched the softness of a ploughed field. He realized that he was no longer on the road. He had gone astray. He could no longer make out which was east or west, which way was the village, the town. The wind whistled, howled, whirled the snow about in eddies. It looked as if white imps were playing tag on the fields. A white dust rose above the ground. Zlateh stopped. She could walk no longer. Stubbornly she anchored her cleft hooves in the earth and bleated as if pleading to be taken home. Icicles hung from her white beard, and her horns were glazed with frost.

Aaron did not want to admit the danger, but he knew just the same that if they did not find shelter they would freeze to death. This was no ordinary storm. It was a mighty blizzard. The snowfall had reached his knees. His hands were numb, and he could no longer feel his toes. He choked when he breathed. His nose felt like wood, and he rubbed it with snow. Zlateh's bleating began to sound like crying. Those humans in whom she had so much confidence had dragged her into a trap. Aaron began to pray to God for himself and for the innocent animal.

Suddenly he made out the shape of a hill. He wondered what it could be. Who had piled snow into such a huge heap? He moved towards it, dragging Zlateh after him. When he came near it, he realized that it was a large haystack which the snow had blanketed.

Aaron saw immediately that they were saved. With great effort he dug his way through the snow. He was a village boy and knew what to do. When he reached the hay, he hollowed out a nest for himself and the goat. No matter how cold it may be outside, in the hay it is always warm. And hay was food for Zlateh. The moment she smelt it she became contented and began to eat. Outside the snow continued to fall. It quickly covered the passageway Aaron had dug. But a boy and an animal need to breathe, and there was hardly any air in their hideout. Aaron bored a kind of window through the hay and snow and carefully kept the passage clear.

Zlateh, having eaten her fill, sat down on her hind legs and seemed to have regained her confidence in man. Aaron ate his two slices of bread and cheese, but after the difficult journey he was still hungry. He looked at Zlateh and noticed her udders were full. He lay down next to her, placing himself so that when he milked her he could squirt the milk into his mouth. It was rich and sweet. Zlateh was not accustomed to being milked that way, but she did not resist. On the contrary, she seemed eager to reward Aaron for bringing her to a shelter whose very walls, floor, and ceiling were made of food.

Through the window Aaron could catch a glimpse of the chaos outside. The wind carried before it whole drifts of snow. It was completely dark, and he did not know whether night had already come or whether it was the darkness of the storm. Thank God that in the hay it was not cold. The dried grass and field flowers exuded the warmth of the summer sun. Zlateh ate frequently; she nibbled from above, below, from the left and right. Her body gave forth an animal warmth, and Aaron cuddled up to her. He had always loved Zlateh, but now she was like a sister. He was alone, cut off from his family, and wanted to talk.

He began to talk to Zlateh. 'Zlateh, what do you think about what has happened to us?' he asked.

'Maaaa,' Zlateh answered.

'If we hadn't found this stack of hay, we would both be frozen stiff by now,' Aaron said.

'Maaaa,' was the goat's reply.

'If the snow keeps on falling like this, we may have to stay here for days,' Aaron explained.

'Maaaa,' Zlateh bleated.

'What does "maaaa" mean?' Aaron asked. 'You'd better speak up clearly.'

'Maaaa. Maaaa,' Zlateh tried.

'Well, let it be "maaaa" then,' Aaron said patiently. 'You can't speak, but I know you understand. I need you and you need me. Isn't that right?'

'Maaaa.'

Aaron became sleepy. He made a pillow out of some hay, leaned his head on it, and dozed off. Zlateh too fell asleep.

When Aaron opened his eyes, he didn't know whether it was morning or night. The snow had blocked up his window. He tried to clear it, but when he had bored through to the length of his arm, he still hadn't reached the outside. Luckily he had his stick with him and was able to break through to the open air. It was still dark outside. The snow continued to fall and the wind wailed, first with one voice and then with many. Sometimes it had the sound of devilish laughter.

Zlateh too awoke, and when Aaron greeted her, she answered, 'Maaaa.' Yes, Zlateh's language consisted of only one word, but it meant many things. Now she was saying, 'We must accept all that God gives us—heat, cold, hunger, satisfaction, light, and darkness.'

Aaron had awakened hungry. He had eaten up his food, but Zlateh had plenty of milk.

For three days Aaron and Zlateh stayed in the haystack. Aaron had always loved Zlateh, but in these three days he loved her more and more. She fed him with her milk and helped him keep warm. She comforted him with her patience. He told her many stories, and she always cocked her ears and listened. When he patted her, she licked his hand and his face. Then she said, 'Maaaa,' and he knew it meant, I love you too.

The snow fell for three days, though after the first day it was not as thick and the wind quieted down. Sometimes Aaron felt that there could never have been a summer, that the snow had always fallen, ever since he could remember. He, Aaron, never had a father or mother or sisters.

He was a snow child, born of the snow, and so was Zlateh. It was so quiet in the hay that his ears rang in the stillness. Aaron and

Zlateh slept all night and a good part of the day. As for Aaron's dreams, they were all about warm weather. He dreamed of green fields, trees covered with blossoms, clear brooks, and singing birds.

By the third night the snow had stopped, but Aaron did not dare to find his way home in the darkness. The sky became clear and the moon shone, casting silvery nets on the snow. Aaron dug his way out and looked at the world. It was all white, quiet, dreaming dreams of heavenly splendour. The stars were large and close. The moon swam in the sky as in a sea.

On the morning of the fourth day Aaron heard the ringing of sleigh bells. The haystack was not far from the road. The peasant who drove the sleigh pointed out the way to him—not to the town and Feyvel the butcher, but home to the village. Aaron had decided in the haystack that he would never part with Zlateh.

Aaron's family and their neighbours had searched for the boy and the goat but had found no trace of them during the storm. They feared they were lost. Aaron's mother and sisters cried for him; his father remained silent and gloomy. Suddenly one of the neighbours came running to their house with the news that Aaron and Zlateh were coming up the road.

There was great joy in the family. Aaron told them how he had found the stack of hay and how Zlateh had fed him with her milk. Aaron's sisters kissed and hugged Zlateh and gave her a special treat of chopped carrots and potato peel, which Zlateh gobbled up hungrily.

Nobody ever again thought of selling Zlateh, and now that the cold weather had finally set in, the villagers needed the services of Reuven the furrier once more. When Hanukkah came, Aaron's mother was able to fry pancakes every evening, and Zlateh got her portion too.

Even though Zlateh had her own pen, she often came to the kitchen, knocking on the door with her horns to indicate that she was ready to visit, and she was always admitted. In the evening Aaron, Miriam, and Anna played dreidel. Zlateh sat near the stove watching the children and the flickering of the Hanukkah candles.

Once in a while Aaron would ask her, 'Zlateh, do you remember the three days we spent together?'

And Zlateh would scratch her neck with a horn, shake her white bearded head and come out with the single sound which expressed all her thoughts, and all her love.

The Pied Piper of Hamelin

Rats! There was a ruin of rats. A rat-attack! A plague of rats. Sidling along streets; scavenging in shops; high-tailing around houses. No one in Hamelin knew what to do about them.

To begin with, there were only a few more than usual. As if the town-rats had simply invited their friends from upriver and downriver to come and have a look round Hamelin.

But then there were a lot more than usual, as if all those friends had decided to stay on, and before long invited their friends.

People began to complain. They didn't like the sight of them, always scurrying round corners, or the smell of them, so sour and strong. And they didn't like the sound of them, squeaking and scritching-and-scratching in every single house.

How fast they were on their feet! They bit the hind-legs of dogs ten times their size; they buried their teeth in the throats of cats; and they actually nipped babies in their cradles.

From the corners of kitchens, they grinned at cooks and then sprang up and licked their soup-ladles; they nose-dived under larder doors, and gnawed their way into the casks of salted sprat and salted herring; they chewed the rims of cheeses; then they curled up their tails, and nested inside men's Sunday hats.

Rats! There was a ruin of rats. A rat-attack! A plague of rats.

At last the people of Hamelin marched to the Town Hall. They were shouting. They were chanting. They were carrying banners with words painted on them: RATS OUT! and I SMELL A RAT; and also, more worryingly for the mayor, I SMELL A MAYOR.

The mayor wasn't a rat. He was such a knickerbockered dumpling he couldn't have scampered anywhere to save his life; and his eyes weren't small or beady but large and grey and somehow faded; but he did have a fur coat—a brown velvet gown lined with white ermine. And so did all the councillors.

'We paid for those gowns,' shouted one man.

'And we'll have them off your backs,' called another.

'Rats! What are you going to do about them?'

'Get rid of them!'

'You're useless!'

'Disgraceful!'

The mayor and the councillors could see that, unless they got rid of the rats, they would never be elected again. But what were they to do? The town ratcatcher had laid traps and sprinkled poison and, true, he had caught a few dozen rats. But you can't catch a whole army any more than you can catch a rainstorm in a pail. So what were they to do?

For more than an hour the mayor and councillors sat in council.

They sat in silence and rocked to and fro and racked their brains.

'Oh! My head aches,' said the mayor. 'It's all very well. All very well!'

At noon, the mayor's stomach invited him to stop thinking about rats. It told him it was time to think about a large bowl of thick green turtle soup.

'Good idea!' murmured the mayor, and his eyes brightened.

At that moment, there was a gentle but firm rat-a-tat-tat at the great oak door of the council chamber.

The mayor gave a start. 'Oh dear!' he said, and he fanned himself with his right hand. 'Anything like that and—and I think it's a rat.' Using his elbows, the mayor levered himself upright in his carved mayoral chair. 'Come in!' he cried.

In came the strangest-looking figure. In and straight up to the mayor. He was wrapped in a gown so long he could have trapped its hem under his heels, and this gown was half yellow and half red: a marvel, a swaying jigsaw of crescents and diamonds, full-moons and coffins and zigzags and squares.

The man himself was tall and thin, with green and blue eyes. He had one of those seamless, hairless, almost ageless faces, and might have been thirty or fifty or even seventy years old.

The man smiled at the mayor and, so it seemed to them, at each of the councillors—little, quick elfin smiles.

'Please, your honours,' said the man. 'Please and listen.'

'Go on!' said the mayor.

'And hurry up about it, man!' said the mayor's stomach.

'I may be able to help you,' said the man. 'I have a special skill! I can make every creature under the sun follow me.'

'Follow you?' said the mayor.

'Every creature that creeps or runs or swims or flies. I've led away armies of moles and toads and vipers. Do you understand?'

'I follow you,' said the mayor.

'And people call me the Pied Piper,' said the man, holding up his hands and trilling his fingers.

Then for the first time the mayor and councillors of Hamelin noticed that the man was wearing a red-and-yellow sash round his neck, with a little reed pipe dangling from it.

'You see!' said the man, smiling. 'Now please and listen! Last June I saved the Cham of Tartary from a terrible swarm of gnats.'

'You did?' said the councillors.

'They were whining around his whiskers,' said the Piper.

'Pickled pepper!' said the mayor.

'And in Asia,' said the Piper, 'I rescued the Nizam from a brood of vampire-bats. So as you see: I can rid Hamelin of your plague of rats.'

'You can?' said the mayor. 'How much? I mean: how much?'

'One thousand guilders.'

'One thousand!' exclaimed the mayor. 'One! We'll give you fifty thousand—and cheap at the price.'

The Piper smiled another little, quick smile and bowed. Then he sailed out of the Town Hall, followed by the mayor and the councillors. Down in the street, the Piper waited until quite a crowd had gathered around him, curious to see what he would do. Then he raised his reed pipe and pursed his lips; his blue-green eyes were dancing.

As soon as the Piper began to play, there was a far-off sound, like a sound at the back of your mind, or the sound of the distant sea. But this hum became a mutter, and the mutter a grumble, and the grumble a rumble, as rats jumped down from barrels and ran along rafters and drummed over floorboards and tumbled downstairs, hundreds of rats, thousands of them, all eager to join the dance.

There were black rats and brown rats and some black-and-tans. Mothers and fathers and squeaking friskers. Grey-faced grandparents. Thick-waisted uncles and stern aunts with whiskers!

The Piper advanced from street to street, and he never stopped piping, not for one moment. He danced the rats all the way round Hamelin and then he led them down to the river. The Piper walked straight into the water and the rats followed him. They all dived in and drowned in the River Weser—all except one.

This one rat swam right across the river. He ran back to Ratland, and when he got there, he told the other rats: 'That music! What music! When the Piper started to play, I heard a sigh of bread rising in the oven and the hiss of fresh milk squirting into the pail; I heard the seething of damson jam; I heard corks popping and bacon crackling; I heard bubble-and-squeak! I heard a sweet, sweet voice telling me to eat and drink and eat—and at that moment, I found myself up to my neck in cold water.'

Then all the people of Hamelin began to gather in the market-place and the church bells rang. They rang and rang until the steeple rocked.

The mayor was purple in the face with pleasure. 'Get sticks!' he shouted. 'Get long poles! Poke out their holy nests! Block up their poky holes! I don't want a trace of them left in Hamelin.'

Then the Piper sauntered into the market-place. 'But first, your honour,' he said, 'please and pay me my one thousand guilders.'

'One thousand guilders!' exclaimed the mayor, and he turned from purple to blue.

'One thousand!' murmured the councillors. 'We can't afford a thousand. What about our council dinners?'

'Mmm!' murmured the mayor. 'We could buy a butt of Rhine wine for half that amount.'

'And then there's the claret and the Graves and the Moselle.'

'Exactly!' said the mayor. He rubbed his nose and then he winked at the councillors. 'Well!' he said. 'The rats are drowned and dead, and the dead can't come back to life, can they!' The mayor wagged a finger at the Piper. 'A thousand indeed! We were only joking, and you know it. But fair's fair: we'll give you a decent bottle, and here—take fifty guilders!'

'Don't you play around with me!' said the Piper, and his eyes shone blue and green, like candle-flames sprinkled with salt. 'I'm in a hurry. I've promised to be in Baghdad in time for supper.'

'Baghdad!' cried the mayor.

'The caliph's cook is making me a bowl of his best stew. I rid his kitchen of a nest of scorpions, and that's all he can afford.'

The mayor turned puce. He began to fan himself with his right hand.

'I didn't drive a hard bargain with him,' said the Piper, 'but I won't let you off—not one penny. And I'll tell you this: if you anger me, I'll pipe another kind of tune.'

'Are you telling me you've charged that cook a bowl of stew, and you're asking us for a thousand guilders?' demanded the mayor. 'I'm not going to be insulted by you—you piebald gypsy! How dare you threaten me? You can blow on your pipe until you balloon! Blow until you burst!'

The Piper raised his reed pipe and pursed his lips; and before he had blown three notes, there was a far-off sound, like the sound of wind in the high tree-tops. But this rustling became a bustling, and the bustling a hustling, as dozens and dozens of children burst into the market-place. Scampering and skipping and shouting and laughing, they thronged around the Piper, all of them eager to join the dance.

There were boys. There were girls. Brothers, half-brothers, sisters, step-sisters. There were little tiny creatures, who had only just learned to walk. And last, a moon-faced boy, whose right leg was all crooked.

Then the Piper stepped out of the market-place, and he never stopped piping, not for one moment. Hopping and clapping, quickstepping, chattering, the children of Hamelin followed him. Their clogs clattered on the cobblestones.

But the mayor and the councillors: they were spellbound. The magical music that made the children dance and sing silenced them and rooted them to the spot. They couldn't move; they couldn't even shout warnings.

The Pied Piper danced the children all the way round Hamelin and then, to the terror of the mayor and councillors, he led them down to the river.

The Weser slipped and slapped against its banks. It sang happy and sad, it echoed the death-songs of all the drowned rats.

Right at the water's edge, the Piper turned aside. He set off down the path along the river-bank, and all the children danced after him. They left Hamelin behind, and crossed the July meadows, and reached the foot of basking Koppelberg.

The hill was steep, the path was steep. But just as it seemed the Piper and children could climb no further, a green door swung open in the side of the hill. The Piper didn't pause. No! With a little, quick smile he walked straight in, and all the children of Hamelin stepped in after him.

All? All except one. The boy with the crooked leg couldn't

dance. He was still way below, calling out to his friends, dragging himself up the stony path.

Then the green door swung shut again, and the moon-faced boy was left on the hillside. He stared and stared; then he folded on to his hands and knees.

The spluttering mayor and councillors sent town messengers north and south and east and west, with instructions to offer the Piper as much silver and gold as he wanted, if only he would bring the children back to Hamelin. But where had he gone? Where were the children? Time passed.

The men and women of Hamelin wept for their sons and daughters. They named the track that runs along the river-bank Pied Piper Street. They cut a story in stone. They painted a church window. Time passed.

Time passed and the moon-faced boy pressed his palms to the earth and stood up on Koppelberg.

'That music!' he said. 'What music! When the Piper started to play, I heard him promise and promise me: a happy land, right next to the town, where rainbows dance in waterfalls and horses have eagles' wings and nothing is not strange. The pear-trees and plum-trees are always in fruit! The roses never fade! And I promise and promise you: your foot will soon be cured.'

The boy's mouth tightened. His friends! His sharings and secret dreams and games and laughter! High on the hill, he left behind his childhood, and began to make his way back to Hamelin.

Stan Bolovan

Once upon a time what happened did happen, and if it had not happened this story would never have been told.

On the outskirts of a village just where the oxen were turned out to pasture, and the pigs roamed about burrowing with their noses among the roots of the trees, there stood a small house. In the house lived a man who had a wife, and the wife was sad all day long.

'Dear wife, what is wrong with you that you hang your head like a drooping rosebud?' asked her husband one morning. 'You have everything you want; why cannot you be merry like other women?'

'Leave me alone, and do not seek to know the reason,' replied she, bursting into tears, and the man thought that it was no time to question her, and went away to his work.

He could not, however, forget all about it, and a few days after he enquired again the reason of her sadness, but only got the same reply. At length he felt he could bear it no longer, and tried a third time, and then his wife turned and answered him.

'Good gracious!' cried she. 'Why cannot you let things be as they are? If I were to tell you, you would become just as wretched as myself. If you would only believe, it is far better for you to know nothing.'

But no man yet was ever content with such an answer. The more you beg him not to enquire, the greater is his curiosity to learn the whole.

'Well, if you must know,' said the wife at last, 'I will tell you. There is no luck in this house—no luck at all!'

'Is not your cow the best milker in all the village? Are not your trees as full of fruit as your hives are full of bees? Has anyone cornfields like ours? Really, you talk nonsense when you say things like that!'

'Yes, all that you say is true, but we have no children.'

Then Stan understood, and when a man once understands and has his eyes opened it is no longer well with him. From that day the little house in the outskirts contained an unhappy man as well as an unhappy woman. And at the sight of her husband's misery the woman became more wretched than ever.

And so matters went on for some time.

Some weeks had passed, and Stan thought he would consult a wise man who lived a day's journey from his own house. The wise man was sitting before his door when he came up, and Stan fell on his knees before him. 'Give me children, my lord, give me children.'

'Take care what you are asking,' replied the wise man. 'Will not children be a burden to you? Are you rich enough to feed and clothe them?'

'Only give them to me, my lord, and I will manage somehow!' and at a sign from the wise man Stan went his way.

He reached home that evening tired and dusty, but with hope in his heart. As he drew near his house a sound of voices struck upon his ear, and he looked up to see the whole place full of children. Children in the garden, children in the yard, children looking out of every window—it seemed to the man as if all the children in the world must be gathered there. And none was bigger than the other, but each was smaller than the other, and every one was more noisy and more impudent and more daring than the rest, and Stan gazed and grew cold with horror as he realized that they all belonged to him.

'Good gracious! How many there are! How many!' he muttered to himself.

'Oh, but not one too many,' smiled his wife, coming up with a crowd more children clinging to her skirts.

But even she found that it was not so easy to look after a hundred children, and when a few days had passed and they had eaten up all the food there was in the house, they began to cry, 'Father! I am hungry—I am hungry,' till Stan scratched his head and wondered what he was to do next. It was not that he thought there were too many children, for his life had seemed more full of joy since they appeared, but now it came to the point he did not know how he was to feed them. The cow had ceased to give milk, and it was too early for the fruit trees to ripen.

'Do you know, old woman,' said he one day to his wife, 'I must go out into the world and try to bring back food somehow, though I cannot tell where it is to come from.'

To the hungry man any road is long, and then there was always the thought that he had to satisfy a hundred greedy children as well as himself.

Stan wandered, and wandered, and wandered, till he reached to the end of the world, where that which is, is mingled with that which is not, and there he saw, a little way off, a sheepfold, with seven sheep in it. In the shadow of some trees lay the rest of the flock.

Stan crept up, hoping that he might manage to decoy some of them away quietly, and drive them home for food for his family, but he soon found this could not be. For at midnight he heard a rushing noise, and through the air flew a dragon, who drove apart a ram, a sheep, and a lamb, and three fine cattle that were lying down close by. And besides these he took the milk of seventy-seven sheep, and carried it home to his old mother, that she might bathe in it and grow young again. And this happened every night.

The shepherd bewailed himself in vain: the dragon only laughed, and Stan saw that this was not the place to get food for his family.

But though he quite understood that it was almost hopeless to fight against such a powerful monster, yet the thought of the hungry children at home clung to him like a burr, and would not be shaken off, and at last he said to the shepherd, 'What will you give me if I rid you of the dragon?'

'One of every three rams, one of every three sheep, one of every three lambs,' answered the herd.

'It is a bargain,' replied Stan, though at the moment he did not know how, supposing he *did* come off the victor, he would ever be able to drive so large a flock home.

However, that matter could be settled later. At present night was not far off, and he must consider how best to fight with the dragon.

Just at midnight, a horrible feeling that was new and strange to him came over Stan—a feeling that he could not put into words even to himself, but which almost forced him to give up the battle and take the shortest road home again. He half turned; then he remembered the children, and turned back.

'You or I,' said Stan to himself, and took up his position on the edge of the flock. 'Stop!' he suddenly cried, as the air was filled with a rushing noise, and the dragon came dashing past.

'Dear me!' exclaimed the dragon, looking round. 'Who are you, and where do you come from?'

'I am Stan Bolovan, who eats rocks all night, and in the day feeds on the flowers of the mountain; and if you meddle with those sheep I will carve a cross on your back.'

When the dragon heard these words he stood quite still in the middle of the road, for he knew he had met with his match.

'But you will have to fight me first,' he said in a trembling voice, for when you faced him properly he was not brave at all.

'I fight you?' replied Stan. 'Why, I could slay you with one breath!' Then, stooping to pick up a large cheese which lay at his feet, he added, 'Go and get a stone like this out of the river, so that we may lose no time in seeing who is the best man.'

The dragon did as Stan bade him, and brought back a stone out of the brook.

'Can you get buttermilk out of your stone?' asked Stan.

The dragon picked up his stone with one hand, and squeezed it till it fell into powder, but no buttermilk flowed from it. 'Of course I can't!' he said, half angrily.

'Well, if you can't, I can,' answered Stan, and he pressed the cheese till buttermilk flowed through his fingers.

When the dragon saw that, he thought it was time he made the best of his way home again, but Stan stood in his path.

'We have still some accounts to settle,' said he, 'about what you have been doing here,' and the poor dragon was too frightened to stir, lest Stan should slay him at one breath and bury him among the flowers in the mountain pastures.

'Listen to me,' he said at last. 'I see you are a very useful person, and my mother has need of a fellow like you. Suppose you enter her service for three days, which are as long as one of your years, and she will pay you each day seven sacks full of ducats.'

Three times seven sacks full of ducats! The offer was very tempting, and Stan could not resist it. He did not waste words, but nodded to the dragon, and they started along the road.

It was a long, long way, but when they came to the end they found the dragon's mother, who was as old as time itself, expecting them. Stan saw her eyes shining like lamps from afar, and when they entered the house they beheld a huge kettle standing on the fire, filled with milk. When the old mother found that her son had arrived empty-handed she grew very angry, and fire and flame darted from her nostrils, but before she could speak the dragon turned to Stan.

'Stay here,' said he, 'and wait for me; I am going to explain things to my mother.'

Stan was already repenting bitterly that he had ever come to such a place, but, since he was there, there was nothing for it but to take everything quietly, and not show that he was afraid.

'Listen, mother,' said the dragon as soon as they were alone, 'I have brought this man in order to get rid of him. He is a terrific fellow who eats rocks, and can press buttermilk out of a stone,' and he told her all that had happened the night before.

'Oh, just leave him to me!' she said. 'I have never yet let a man slip through my fingers.' So Stan had to stay and do the old mother service.

The next day she told him that he and her son should try which was the strongest, and she took down a huge club, bound seven times with iron.

The dragon picked it up as if it had been a feather, and, after whirling it round his head, flung it lightly three miles away, telling Stan to beat that if he could.

They walked to the spot where the club lay. Stan stooped and felt it; then a great fear came over him, for he knew that he and all his children together would never lift that club from the ground.

'What are you doing?' asked the dragon.

'I was thinking what a beautiful club it was, and what a pity it is that it should cause your death.'

'How do you mean—my death?' asked the dragon.

'Only that I am afraid that if I throw it you will never see another dawn. You don't know how strong I am!'

'Oh, never mind that—be quick and throw.'

'If you are really in earnest, let us go and feast for three days: that will at any rate give you three extra days of life.'

Stan spoke so calmly that this time the dragon began to get a little frightened, though he did not quite believe that things would be as bad as Stan said.

They returned to the house, took all the food that could be found in the old mother's larder, and carried it back to the place where the club was lying. Then Stan seated himself on the sack of provisions, and remained quietly watching the setting moon.

'What are you doing?' asked the dragon.

'Waiting till the moon gets out of my way.'

'What do you mean? I don't understand.'

'Don't you see that the moon is exactly in my way? But of

course, if you like, I will throw the club into the moon.'

At these words the dragon grew uncomfortable for the second time. He prized the club, which had been left him by his grandfather, very highly, and had no desire that it should be lost in the moon.

'I'll tell you what,' he said, after thinking a little. 'Don't throw the club at all. I will throw it a second time, and that will do just as well.'

'No, certainly not!' replied Stan. 'Just wait till the moon sets.'

But the dragon, in dread lest Stan should fulfil his threats, tried what bribes could do, and in the end had to promise Stan seven sacks of ducats before he was suffered to throw back the club himself.

'Oh, dear me, that is indeed a strong man,' said the dragon, turning to his mother. 'Would you believe that I have had the greatest difficulty in preventing him from throwing the club into the moon?'

Then the old woman grew uncomfortable too! Only to think of it! It was no joke to throw things into the moon! So no more was heard of the club, and the next day they all had something else to think about.

'Go and fetch me water!' said the mother, when the morning broke, and gave them twelve buffalo skins with the order to keep filling them till night.

They set out at once for the brook, and in the twinkling of an eye the dragon had filled the whole twelve, carried them into the house, and brought them back to Stan. Stan was tired: he could scarcely lift the buckets when they were empty, and he shuddered to think of what would happen when they were full.

But he only took an old knife out of his pocket and began to scratch up the earth near the brook.

'What are you doing there? How are you going to carry the water into the house?' asked the dragon.

'How? Dear me, that is easy enough! I shall just take the brook!'

At these words the dragon's jaw dropped. This was the last thing that had ever entered his head, for the brook had been as it was since the days of his grandfather.

'I'll tell you what!' he said. 'Let me carry your skins for you.'

'Most certainly not,' answered Stan, going on with his digging, and the dragon, in dread lest he should fulfil his threat, tried what bribes would do, and in the end had again to promise seven sacks of ducats before Stan would agree to leave the brook alone and let him carry the water into the house.

On the third day the old mother sent Stan into the forest for wood, and, as usual, the dragon went with him.

Before you could count three he had pulled up more trees than Stan could have cut down in a lifetime, and had arranged them neatly in rows. When the dragon had finished, Stan began to look about him, and, choosing the biggest of the trees, he climbed up it, and, breaking off a long rope of wild vine, bound the top of the tree to the one next it. And so he did to a whole line of trees.

'What are you doing there?' asked the dragon.

'You can see for yourself,' answered Stan, going quietly on with his work.

'Why are you tying the trees together?'

'Not to give myself unnecessary work; when I pull up one, all the others will come up too.'

'But how will you carry them home?'

'Dear me! Don't you understand that I am going to take the whole forest back with me?' said Stan, tying two other trees as he spoke.

'I'll tell you what,' cried the dragon, trembling with fear at the thought of such a thing, 'let me carry the wood for you, and you shall have seven times seven sacks full of ducats.'

'You are a good fellow, and I agree to your proposal,' answered Stan, and the dragon carried the wood.

Now the three days' service which were to be reckoned as a year were over, and the only thing that disturbed Stan was, how to get all those ducats back to his home!

In the evening the dragon and his mother had a long talk, but Stan heard every word through a crack in the ceiling.

'Woe be to us, mother,' said the dragon, 'this man will soon get us into his power. Give him his money, and let us be rid of him.'

But the old mother was fond of money, and did not like this.

'Listen to me,' she said. 'You must murder him this very night.'

'I am afraid,' answered he.

'There is nothing to fear,' replied the old mother. 'When he is asleep take the club, and hit him on the head with it. It is easily done.'

And so it would have been, had not Stan heard all about it.

And when the dragon and his mother had put out their lights, he took the pigs' trough and filled it with earth, and placed it in his bed, and covered it with clothes. Then he hid himself underneath, and began to snore loudly.

Very soon the dragon stole softly into the room, and gave a tremendous blow on the spot where Stan's head should have been. Stan groaned loudly from under the bed, and the dragon went away as softly as he had come. Directly he had closed the door, Stan lifted out the pigs' trough, and lay down himself, after making everything clean and tidy, but he was wise enough not to shut his eyes that night.

The next morning he came into the room when the dragon and his mother were having their breakfast.

'Good morning,' said he.

'Good morning. How did you sleep?'

'Oh, very well, but I dreamed that a flea had bitten me, and I seem to feel it still.'

The dragon and his mother looked at each other. 'Do you hear that?' whispered he. 'He talks of a flea. I broke my club on his head.'

This time the mother grew as frightened as her son. There was nothing to be done with a man like this, and she made all haste to fill the sacks with ducats, so as to get rid of Stan as soon as possible.

But on his side Stan was trembling like an aspen, as he could not lift even one sack from the ground. So he stood still and looked at them.

'What are you standing there for?' asked the dragon.

'Oh, I was standing here because it has just occurred to me that I should like to stay in your service for another year. I am ashamed that when I get home they should see I have brought back so little. I know that they will cry out, "Just look at Stan Bolovan, who in one year has grown as weak as a dragon."'

Here a shriek of dismay was heard both from the dragon and his mother, who declared they would give him seven or even seven times seven the number of sacks if he would only go away.

'I'll tell you what!' said Stan at last. 'I see you don't want me to stay, and I should be very sorry to make myself disagreeable. I will go at once, but only on condition that you shall carry the money home yourself, so that I may not be put to shame before my friends.'

The words were hardly out of his mouth before the dragon had snatched up the sacks and piled them on his back. Then he and Stan set forth.

The way, though really not far, was yet too long for Stan, but at length he heard his children's voices, and stopped short. He did not wish the dragon to know where he lived, lest some day he should come to take back his treasure. Was there nothing he could say to get rid of the monster? Suddenly an idea came into Stan's head, and he turned round.

'I hardly know what to do,' said he. 'I have a hundred children, and I am afraid they may do you harm, as they are always ready for a fight. However, I will do my best to protect you.'

A hundred children! That was indeed no joke! The dragon let fall the sacks from terror, and then picked them up again. But the children, who had had nothing to eat since their father had left them, came rushing towards him, waving knives in their right hands and forks in their left, and crying, 'Give us dragon's flesh; we will have dragon's flesh.'

At this dreadful sight the dragon waited no longer: he flung down his sacks where he stood and took flight as fast as he could, so terrified at the fate that awaited him that from that day he has never dared to show his face in the world again.

The Dead Man's Nightcap

On a farm beside a church there lived, among others, a young boy and a girl. The boy made a habit of scaring the girl, but she had got so used to it that she was never frightened of anything, for if she did see something she thought it was the boy trying to scare her.

One day it so happened that the washing had been done, and that among the things there were many white nightcaps, such as were in fashion then. In the evening the girl was told to fetch in the washing, which was out in the churchyard. She runs out, and begins to pick up the washing. When she has almost finished, she sees a white spectre sitting on one of the graves. She thinks to herself that the lad is planning to scare her, so she runs up and snatches the spectre's cap off (for she thought the boy had taken one of the nightcaps) and says: 'Now don't you start trying to scare me this time!'

So she went indoors with the washing; the boy had been indoors the whole time. They started sorting out the washing; there was one nightcap too many now, and it was earthy on the inside. Then the girl was scared.

Next morning the spectre was still sitting on the grave, and people did not know what to do about it, as nobody dared take the cap back, and so they sent word all round the district, asking for advice. There was one old man in the district who declared that it would be impossible to stop something bad coming of it, unless the girl herself took the cap back to the spectre and placed it on its head in silence, and that there ought to be many people there to watch.

The girl was forced to go with the cap and place it on the spectre's head, and so she went, though her heart was not much in it, and she placed the cap on the head of the spectre, and when she had done so she said, 'Are you satisfied now?'

But at this the dead man started to his feet, struck her, and said, 'Yes! And you, are you satisfied?'

And with these words he plunged down into the grave. The girl fell down at the blow, and when men ran to pick her up, she was already dead. The boy was punished because he used to scare her, for it was considered that the whole unfortunate affair had been his fault, and he gave up scaring people. And that is the end of this tale.

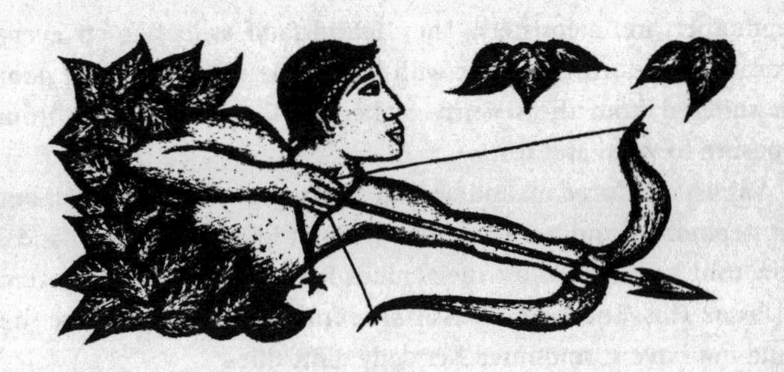

Vasilissa the Fair

A merchant and his wife living in a certain country had an only daughter, the beautiful Vasilissa. When the child was eight years old the mother was seized with a fatal illness, but before she died she called Vasilissa to her side and, giving her a little doll, said, 'Listen, dear daughter. Remember my last words. I am dying, and bequeath to you now, together with a parent's blessing, this doll. Keep it always beside you, but show it to nobody; if at any time you are in trouble, give the doll some food and ask its advice.' Then the mother kissed her daughter, sighed deeply and died.

After his wife's death the merchant grieved for a long time, and next began to think whether he should not wed again. He was handsome and would have no difficulty in finding a bride; moreover, he was especially pleased with a certain little widow, no longer young, who possessed two daughters of about the same age as Vasilissa.

The widow was famous as both a good housekeeper and a good mother to her daughters, but when the merchant married her he quickly found she was unkind to his daughter. Vasilissa, being the chief beauty in the village, was on that account envied by her stepmother and stepsisters. They found fault with her on every occasion, and tormented her with impossible tasks; thus, the poor girl suffered from the severity of her work and grew dark from exposure to wind and sun.

Vasilissa endured all and became every day more beautiful; but the stepmother and her daughters who sat idle with folded hands, grew thin and almost lost their minds from spite. What supported Vasilissa? This. She received assistance from her doll; otherwise she could not have surmounted her daily difficulties.

Vasilissa, as a rule, kept a dainty morsel for her doll, and in the evening when everyone had gone to bed she would steal to her closet and regale her doll and say, 'Now, dear, eat and listen to my grief! Though I am living in my father's house, my life is joyless; a wicked stepmother makes me wretched; please direct my life and tell me what to do.'

The doll tasted the food, and gave advice to the sorrowing child, and in the morning performed her work, so that Vasilissa could rest in the shade or pluck flowers; already the beds had been weeded, and the cabbages watered, and the water carried, and the stove heated. It was nice for Vasilissa to live with her doll.

Several years passed. Vasilissa grew up, and the young men in the town sought her hand in marriage; but they never looked at the stepsisters. Growing more angry than ever, the stepmother answered Vasilissa's suitors thus: 'I will not let you have my youngest daughter before her sisters.' She dismissed the suitors and vented her spite on Vasilissa with harsh words and blows.

But it happened that the merchant was obliged to visit a neighbouring country, where he had business; and in the meanwhile the stepmother went to live in a house situated close to a thick forest. In the forest was a glade, in which stood a cottage, and in the cottage lived Baba-Yaga, who admitted nobody to her cottage, and devoured people as if they were chickens.

Having moved to the new house, the merchant's wife continually, on some pretext or other, sent the hated Vasilissa into the forest, but the girl always returned home safe and unharmed, because the doll directed her and took care she did not enter Baba-Yaga's cottage.

Spring arrived, and the stepmother assigned to each of the three girls an evening task; thus, she set one to make lace, a second to knit stockings, and Vasilissa to spin. One evening, having extinguished all the lights in the house except one candle in the room where the girls sat at work, the stepmother went to bed. In a little while the candle needed attention, and one of the stepmother's daughters took the snuffers and, beginning to cut the wick, as if by accident, put out the light.

'What are we to do now?' said the girls. 'There is no light in the whole house, and our tasks are unfinished; someone must run for a light to Baba-Yaga.'

'I can see my pins,' said the daughter who was making lace. 'I shall not go.'

'Neither shall I,' said the daughter who was knitting stockings. 'My needles are bright.'

'You must run for a light. Go to Baba-Yaga's,' they both cried, pushing Vasilissa from the room.

Vasilissa went to her closet, placed some supper ready for the doll, and said, 'Now, little doll, have something to eat and hear my trouble. They have sent me to Baba-Yaga's for a light, and she will eat me.'

'Do not be afraid!' answered the doll. 'Go on your errand, but take me with you. No harm will befall you while I am present.' Vasilissa placed the doll in her pocket, crossed herself and entered the thick forest, but she trembled.

Suddenly a horseman galloped past; he was white and dressed in white, his steed was white and had a white saddle and bridle. The morning light was appearing.

The girl went further and another horseman rode past; he was red and dressed in red and his steed was red. The sun rose.

Vasilissa walked all night and all day, but on the following evening she came out in a glade, where stood Baba-Yaga's cottage. The fence around the cottage was made of human bones, and on the fence there were fixed human skulls with eyes. Instead of doorposts at the gates there were human legs; instead of bolts there were hands, instead of a lock there was a mouth with sharp teeth. Vasilissa grew pale from terror and stood as if transfixed.

Suddenly another horseman rode up; he was black and dressed in black and upon a black horse; he sprang through Baba-Yaga's gates and vanished, as if he had been hurled into the earth. Night came on. But the darkness did not last long; the eyes in all the skulls on the fence lighted up, and at once it became as light throughout the glade as if it were midday. Vasilissa trembled from fear, and not knowing whither to run, she remained motionless.

Suddenly she heard a terrible noise. The trees cracked, the dry leaves rustled, and out of the forest Baba-Yaga appeared, riding in a mortar which she drove with a pestle, while she swept away traces of her progress with a broom. She came up to the gates and stopped; then sniffing about her, cried, 'Phoo, phoo, I smell a Russian! Who is here?'

Vasilissa approached the old woman timidly and gave her a low bow; then she said, 'It is I, granny! My stepsisters have sent me to you for a light.'

'Very well,' said Baba-Yaga, 'I know them. If you first of all live with me and do some work, then I will give you a light. If you refuse, I will eat you.' Then she turned to the gates and exclaimed, 'Strong bolts, unlock; wide gates, open!' The gates opened, and Baba-Yaga went in whistling. Vasilissa followed, and all again closed.

Having entered the room, the witch stretched herself and said to Vasilissa, 'Hand me everything in the oven; I am hungry.' Vasilissa lit a torch from the skulls upon the fence and, drawing the food from the oven, handed it to the witch. The meal would have been sufficient for ten men. Moreover, Vasilissa brought up from the cellar kvass, and honey, and beer and wine. The old woman ate and drank almost everything. She left nothing for Vasilissa but some fragments, end-crusts of bread and tiny morsels of sucking pig.

Baba-Yaga lay down to sleep and said, 'When I go away tomorrow, take care that you clean the yard, sweep out the cottage, cook the dinner and get ready the linen. Then go to the cornbin, take a quarter of the wheat and cleanse it from impurities. See that all is done, otherwise I shall eat you.'

After giving these injunctions Baba-Yaga began to snore. But Vasilissa placed the remains of the old woman's meal before her doll and, bursting into tears, said, 'Now, little doll, take some food and hear my grief. Baba-Yaga has set me a terrible task, and has threatened to eat me if I fail in any way; help me!'

The doll answered, 'Have no fear, beautiful Vasilissa! Eat your supper, say your prayers and lie down to sleep; morning is wiser than evening.'

It was early when Vasilissa woke, but Baba-Yaga, who had already risen, was looking out of the window. Suddenly the light from the eyes in the skulls was extinguished; then a pale horseman flashed by, and it was altogether daylight. Baba-Yaga went out and whistled; a mortar appeared before her with a pestle and a hearth broom. A red horseman flashed by, and the sun rose. Then Baba-Yaga took her place in the mortar and went forth, driving herself with the pestle and sweeping away traces of her progress with the broom.

Vasilissa remained alone and, eyeing Baba-Yaga's house, wondered at her wealth. The girl did not know which task to begin with. But when she looked she found that the work was already done: the doll had separated from the wheat the last grains of impurity.

'Oh, my dear liberator,' said Vasilissa to the doll, 'you have rescued me from misfortune!'

'You have only to cook the dinner,' said the doll, climbing into Vasilissa's pocket. 'God help you to prepare it; then rest in peace!'

Towards evening Vasilissa laid the table and awaited Baba-Yaga's return. It became dusk, and a black horseman flashed by the gates; it had grown altogether dark. But the eyes in the skulls shone and the trees cracked and the leaves rustled. Baba-Yaga came. Vasilissa met her. 'Is all done?' asked the witch.

'Look for yourself, granny!'

Baba-Yaga examined everything and, vexed that she had no cause for anger, said, 'My true servants, my bosom friends, grind my wheat!' Three pairs of hands appeared, seized the wheat and bore it from sight.

Baba-Yaga ate to repletion, prepared for sleep, and again gave an order to Vasilissa. 'Tomorrow repeat your task of today; in addition remove the poppies from the cornbin and cleanse them from earth, seed by seed; you see, someone has maliciously mixed earth with them!' Having spoken, the old woman turned to the wall and snored.

Vasilissa began to feed her doll, who said, as on the previous day, 'Pray to God and go to sleep; morning is wiser than evening; all will be done, dear Vasilissa!'

In the morning Baba-Yaga departed again in her mortar, and immediately Vasilissa and the doll set to work at their tasks. The old woman returned, observed everything and cried out, 'My faithful servants, my close friends, squeeze the oil from the poppies!' Three pairs of hands seized the poppies and bore them from sight. Baba-Yaga sat down to dine, and Vasilissa stood silent.

'Why do you say nothing?' remarked the witch. 'You stand as if you were dumb.'

Timidly Vasilissa replied, 'If you would permit me, I should like to ask you a question.'

'Ask, but remember, not every question leads to good. You will learn much; you will soon grow old.'

'I only wish to ask you,' said the girl, 'about what I have seen. When I came to you a pale horseman dressed in white on a white horse overtook me. Who was he?'

'He is my clear day,' answered Baba-Yaga.

'Then another horseman, who was red and dressed in red, and who rode a red horse, overtook me. Who was he?'

'He was my little red sun!' was the answer.

'But who was the black horseman who passed me at the gate, granny?'

'He was my dark night; all three are my faithful servants.'

Vasilissa recalled the three pairs of hands, but was silent.

'Have you nothing more to ask?' said Baba-Yaga.

'I have, but you said, granny, that I shall learn much as I grow older.'

'It is well,' answered the witch, 'that you have enquired only about things outside and not about anything here! I do not like my rubbish to be carried away, and I eat over-inquisitive people! Now I will ask you something. How did you succeed in performing the tasks which I set you?'

'My mother's blessing assisted me,' answered Vasilissa.

'Depart, favoured daughter! I do not require people who have been blessed.' Baba-Yaga dragged Vasilissa out of the room and pushed her beyond the gate, took down from the fence a skull with burning eyes and, putting it on a stick, gave it to the girl and said, 'Take this light to your stepsisters; they sent you here for it.'

Vasilissa ran off, the skull giving her light, which only went out in the morning; and at last, on the evening of the second day, she reached home. As she approached the gates, she was on the point of throwing away the skull, for she thought that there would no longer be any need for a light at home. Then suddenly a hollow voice from the skull was heard to say, 'Do not cast me aside, but carry me to your stepmother.' Glancing at the house, and not seeing a light in any of the windows, she decided to enter with the skull.

At first her stepmother and stepsisters met her with caresses, telling her that they had been without a light from the moment of her departure; they could not strike a light in any way, and if anybody brought one from the neighbours, it went out directly it was carried into the room. 'Perhaps your light will last,' said the stepmother. When they carried the skull into the room its eyes shone brightly and looked continually at the stepmother and her daughters. All their efforts to hide themselves were vain; wherever they rushed they were ceaselessly pursued by the eyes, and before dawn had been burnt to ashes, though Vasilissa was unharmed.

In the morning the girl buried the skull in the ground, locked up the house and visited the town, where she asked admission into the home of a certain old woman who was without kindred. Here she lived quietly and awaited her father. But one day she said to the old woman, 'It tires me to sit idle, granny! Go off and buy me some of the best flax; I will busy myself with spinning.'

The old woman purchased the flax and Vasilissa sat down to spin. The work proceeded rapidly, and the thread when spun was as smooth and fine as a small hair. The thread lay in heaps, and it was time to begin weaving, but a weaver's comb could not be found to suit Vasilissa's thread, and nobody would undertake to make one. Then the girl had recourse to her doll, who said, 'Bring me an old comb that has belonged to a weaver, and an old shuttle, and a horse's mane, and I will do everything for you.'

Vasilissa obtained everything necessary, and lay down to sleep. The doll, in a single night, made a first-rate loom. Towards the end of winter linen had been woven of so fine a texture that it could be drawn through the needle where the thread should pass.

In spring the linen was bleached, and Vasilissa said to the old woman, 'Sell this linen, granny, and keep the money for yourself.'

The old woman glanced at the work and said with a sigh, 'Ah! my child, nobody but a tsar would wear such linen. I will take it to the palace.'

She went to the royal dwelling, and walked up and down in front of the windows. When the tsar saw her he said, 'What do you desire, old woman?'

'Your Majesty,' she answered, 'I have brought some wonderful material, and will show it to nobody but yourself.'

The tsar ordered that she should be admitted, and marvelled

when he saw the linen. 'How much do you ask for it?' he enquired.

'It is not for sale, Tsar and Father! I have brought it as a gift.' The tsar thanked her, and sent her away with some presents.

Some shirts for the tsar were cut out from this linen, but a seamstress could nowhere be found to complete them. At last the tsar summoned the old woman and said to her, 'You were able to spin and weave this linen, so you will be able to sew together some shirts from it.'

'Tsar, it was not I who spun and wove the linen; it is the work of a beautiful maiden.'

'Well, let her sew them!'

The old woman returned home and related everything to Vasilissa. The girl said in reply, 'I knew that this work would not pass out of my hands.' She shut herself in her room and began the undertaking; soon, without resting her hands, she had completed a dozen shirts.

The old woman bore them to the tsar, while Vasilissa washed herself and combed her hair, dressed and then took a seat at the window, and there awaited events. She saw a royal servant come to the old woman's house. He entered the room and said, 'The Tsar-Emperor desires to see the skilful worker who made his shirts, and to reward her out of his royal hands.'

Vasilissa presented herself before the tsar. So much did she please him that he said, 'I cannot bear to separate from you; become my wife!' The tsar took her by her white hands, placed her beside himself, and the wedding was celebrated.

Vasilissa's father quickly returned to rejoice at his daughter's good fortune and to live with her. Vasilissa took the old woman into the palace, and never separated from the little doll, which she kept in her pocket.

The Three Blows

Their stone farmhouse seemed to grow out of the grey-green skirt of the mountain. The walls were lichenous, one part of the roof was covered with slate and the other part with turf. The whole building was so low slung it seemed to be crouching.

It wasn't alone. Megan could stand at their door (you had to stoop to get in or out) and see three other small-holdings within reach, almost within shouting distance. And no more than a mile away, along the track north and west, huddled and patient, was the little village of Llanddeusant.

But when the wind opened its throat and rain swept across the slopes; when the lean seasons came to Black Mountain; when wolves circled the pens and small birds left their sanskrit in the snow: the farm seemed alone then, alone in the world—and all the more so to Megan since her husband had died leaving her to bring up their baby son and run the farm on her own.

But Megan was a hard-working woman. As the years passed, her holding of cattle and sheep and goats so increased that they strayed far and wide over Black Mountain. And all the while her son grew and grew until he became a big-boned young man: rather awkward, very strong-willed, and shy and affectionate. Yet sometimes, when she looked at him sitting by the fire, lost in his own sliding dreams, it seemed to Megan that she didn't really quite know her son. He's like his father, she thought. Something hidden. What is he thinking?

Gwyn spent most of his time up on Black Mountain, herding the cattle and sheep and goats. More often than not he followed them up to a remote place in a fold of the mountain: it was a secret eye, a dark pupil that watched the sun and moon and stars: the little lake of Llyn y Fan Fach.

One spring morning, Gwyn was poking along the edge of the lake, on his way to the flat rock where he sometimes sat and spread out his provisions—barley-bread, maybe, and a chump of cheese, a wooden bottle seething with ale. Gwyn clambered on to the rock and stared out across the lake, silver and obsidian. And there, sitting on the glassy surface of the water, combing her hair, he saw a young woman. She was using the water as a mirror, charming her hair into ringlets, arranging them so that they covered her shoulders; and only when she had finished did she look up and see Gwyn, awkward on the rock, open-mouthed, arms stretched out, offering her bread . . .

Slowly, so slowly she scarcely seemed to move at all, the young woman glided over the surface of the water towards Gwyn and, entranced, he stepped down to meet her.

And then Gwyn heard her voice. It was like a bell, heard long ago and remembered: very sweet and very low. 'Your bread's baked and hard,' she said. 'It's not easy to catch me.'

Which is just what Gwyn tried to do. He lunged into the lake, and at once the girl sank from sight; she left her smile behind, playing on the smooth surface of the water.

For a while Gwyn stood and stared. A stray cloud passed in front of the sun; the water shivered. Gwyn felt as if he had found the one thing in this world that mattered only to lose it. And he resolved to come back, to find the girl and catch her, whatever the cost.

Gwyn turned away from the lake. He set off down the string-thin sheep-runs, the network that covered the steep shoulders of the mountain. At first he walked slowly, but by the time he reached the doors of his farmhouse he was almost running, so eager was he to tell his mother about the bewitching girl he had seen up at Llyn y Fan Fach.

'Stuff!' said Megan. 'You and your dreams.' But as she listened to Gwyn, she did not doubt that he was telling the truth. Perhaps she saw in the young man at her hearth another young man at the same hearth long before, shining and stammering. But then she quailed as she thought of what might become of Gwyn if he was caught up with the fairy folk.

'I won't be put off,' said Gwyn. 'I won't be put off if that's what you're thinking.'

'Leave her alone, Gwyn,' said Megan. 'Take a girl from the valley.'

'I won't be put off,' said Gwyn.

'You won't catch her,' Megan said, 'not unless you listen to me.'

'What do you mean?' said Gwyn.

'"Your bread's baked and hard." Isn't that what she said?'

Gwyn nodded.

'Well, then. Take up some toes. Take up some toes. Stands to reason.'

'Toes?' said Gwyn.

'Pieces of dough. Unbaked and just as they are.'

Gwyn followed his mother's advice. As night began to lose its thickness, yet before you could say it was dawn, he filled one pocket with dough, and quietly let himself out of the farmhouse without waking his mother. He sniffed the cool air and began to climb the dun and misty mountain.

She was not there. Shape-changing mist that plays tricks with the eyes dipped and rose and dipped over the dark water until the sun came down from the peaks and burned it away. Birds arrived in boating parties, little fish made circles, and she was not there.

Not long before dusk, Gwyn saw that two of his cows were lumbering straight towards the top of the dangerous escarpment on the far side of the lake. He stood up at once and began to run round the lake after them. 'Stupids!' he bawled. 'You'll lose your footing.'

Then she was there. She was there, sitting on the shimmer of the water, smiling, just as she had done on the day before.

Gwyn stopped. He reached out his arms and, as the beautiful young woman drifted towards him, he gazed at her: the blue-black sheen of her hair, her long fingers, the green watersilk of her dress, and her little ankles and sandals tied with thongs. Then Gwyn dug into his pockets and offered her the unbaked dough and not only that but his hand too and his heart for ever.

'Your bread is unbaked,' said the young woman. 'I will not have you.' Then she raised her arms and sank under the surface of the water.

Gwyn cried out, and the rockface heard and answered him, all hollow and disembodied. But even as he looked at the lake and listened to the sounds, each as mournful as the other, Gwyn thought of the girl's smile and was half-comforted. 'I'll catch you,' he said.

'You caught the cows,' said Megan later that evening. 'That's what matters.'

Gwyn grinned.

'Anyhow,' said Megan, 'you're not going up there again, are you?'

'You know I am,' said Gwyn.

'In that case,' said his mother, 'listen to me. I'd take some partly baked bread up with you.'

Gwyn reached Llyn y Fan Fach again as day dawned. He kept a watch on the lake and his whole face glowed—his cheeks and chin and ears and eyes, above all his eyes—as if he had just turned away from a leaping fire. He felt strong and he felt weak.

This time it was the sheep and goats that strayed towards the rockface and scree at the far end of the lake. But Gwyn knew how nimble-footed they were. Even when they loosened and dislodged a rock that bumped and bundled down the escarpment and splashed into the lake, they were in no danger.

All morning, wayward April shook sheets of sunlight and rain over the lake and then, in the afternoon, the clouds piling in from the west closed over the mountain. For hour after hour, Gwyn crouched on the smooth rock or padded round the rim of the lake. Now he was no longer so excited or fearful; the long waiting had dulled him.

In the early evening, the mood of the weather changed again. First, Gwyn could see blue sky behind the gauze of cloud, and then the clouds left the mountain altogether. The lake and the ashen scree were soothed by yellow sunlight.

This was the hour when Gwyn saw that three cows were walking on the water. They were out in the middle of Llyn y Fan Fach and ambling towards him.

Gwyn stood up. He swung off the rock platform and down to the lakeside. And as he did so, the young woman appeared for the third time, as beautiful as before, passing over the mirror of water just behind the three cows.

Gwyn stepped into the lake, up to his shins, his thighs, his hips. Still the young woman came on, and she was smiling—an expression that lit up her whole face, and above all her violet eyes.

Gwyn reached out his hands and, wordless, offered her the partly baked bread.

The young woman took the bread, and Gwyn grasped her cool hand. He was nervous and breathless.

'Come with me,' he said. 'Come to the farm . . . I'll show you. Come with me . . . marry me!'

The young woman looked at Gwyn.

'I'll not let you go,' said Gwyn. He could hear his voice rising, as if someone else were speaking. 'I've waited!' He tightened his grip on the girl's hand.

'Gwyn,' said the young woman. 'I will marry you,' she said, 'on one condition.'

'Anything!' said Gwyn. 'Anything you ask.'

'I will marry you and live with you. But if you strike me . . .'

'Strike you!' cried Gwyn.

'. . . strike me three blows without reason, I'll return to this lake and you'll never see me again.'

'Never!' swore Gwyn. 'Never!' He loosened his fierce grip and at once she slid away, raised her arms, and disappeared under the surface of the water.

'Come back!' shouted Gwyn. 'Come back!'

'Gon-ba!' said the mountain. 'Gon-ba!'

Gwyn stood up to his waist in the chill water. The huge, red sun alighted on the western horizon and began to slip out of sight.

But now two young women, each as lovely as the other, rose out of the water and a tall old white-headed man immediately after them. At once they came walking towards Gwyn.

'Greetings, Gwyn!' called the old man. 'You mean to marry one of my daughters, you've asked her to marry you.' He waved towards the two girls at his side. 'And I agree to this. You can marry her if you can tell me which one you mean to marry.'

Gwyn looked from one girl to the other: their clefs of black hair, their strange violet eyes, their long necks . . .

One of the girls tossed her charcoal hair; the other eased one foot forward, one inch, two inches, and into Gwyn's memory. The sandals . . . the thongs . . .

Gwyn reached out at once across the water and took her cool hand. 'This is she,' he said.

'You have made your choice?' asked the old man.

'I have,' said Gwyn.

'You've chosen well,' the man said. 'And you can marry her. Be kind to her, and faithful.'

'I will,' said Gwyn, 'and I will.'

'This is her dowry,' said the man. 'She can have as many sheep and cattle and goats and horses as she can count without drawing breath.'

No sooner had her father spoken than his daughter began to count for the sheep. She counted in fives, 'One, two, three, four, five—one, two, three, four, five' over and over again until she'd run out of breath.

'Thirty-two times,' said the man. 'One hundred and sixty sheep.' As soon as they had been named, the sheep appeared on the surface of the darkening water, and ran across it to the bare mountain.

'Now the cattle,' said the old man. Then his daughter began to count again, her voice soft and rippling. And so they went on until there were more than six hundred head of sheep and cattle and goats and horses milling around on the lakeside.

'Go now,' said the white-headed man gently. 'And remember, Gwyn, if you strike her three blows without reason, she'll return to me, and bring all her livestock back to this lake.'

It was almost dark. The old man and his other daughter went down into the lake. Gwyn took his bride's hand and, followed by her livestock, led her down from the mountain.

So Gwyn and the girl from Llan y Fan Fach were married. Gwyn left the house in which he had been born, and his mother in it, and went to a farm a few miles away, outside the village of Myddfai.

Gwyn and his wife were happy and, because of the generosity of the old man, they were rich. They had three sons, dark-haired, dark-eyed, lovely to look at.

Some years after Gwyn and his wife had moved to Myddfai, they were invited to a christening back in Llanddeusant. Gwyn was eager to go but, when the time came for them to set off, his wife was not.

'I don't know these people,' she said.

'It's Gareth,' said Gwyn. 'I've known him all my life. And this is his first child.'

'It's too far to walk,' said his wife.

'Fetch a horse from the field then,' said Gwyn. 'You can ride down.'

'Will you go and find my gloves,' said Gwyn's wife, 'while I get the horse? I left them in the house.'

When Gwyn came out of the farmhouse with the gloves, eager to be off, his wife had made no move towards the paddock and the horse.

'What's wrong?' cried Gwyn, and he slapped his wife's shoulder with one of her gloves.

Gwyn's wife turned to face him. Her eyes darkened. 'Gwyn!' she said. 'Gwyn! Remember the condition on which I married you.'

'I remember,' said Gwyn.

'That you would never strike me without reason.'

Gwyn nodded.

'Be careful! Be more careful from now on!'

Not long after this, Gwyn and his wife went to a fine wedding. The guests at the breakfast came not only from Llanddeusant and Myddfai but many of the surrounding farms and villages. The barn in which the reception was held was filled with the hum of contentment and the sweet sound of the triple harp.

As soon as she had kissed the bride, Gwyn's wife began to weep and then to sob. The guests around her stopped talking. A few tried to comfort her but many backed away, superstitious of tears at a wedding.

Gwyn didn't know quite what to do. 'What's wrong?' he whispered. 'What's wrong?' But his wife sobbed as bitterly as a little child. Gwyn smiled apologetically and shook his head; then he pursed his lips and dropped a hand on to his wife's arm. 'What's the matter?' he insisted. 'You must stop!'

Gwyn's wife gazed at her husband with her flooded violet eyes. 'These two people,' she said, 'are on the threshold of such trouble. I see it all. And Gwyn,' she said, 'I see your troubles are about to begin. You've struck me without reason for the second time.'

Gwyn's wife loved her husband no less than he loved her and neither had the least desire that their marriage should suddenly come to an end. Knowing that her own behaviour could surprise and upset Gwyn, she sometimes reminded her husband to be very careful not to strike her for a third time. 'Otherwise,' she said, 'I must return to Llyn y Fan Fach. I have no choice in the matter.'

But the years passed. The three boys became young men, all of them intelligent. And when he thought about it at all, Gwyn believed that he had learned his lesson on the way to the christening and at the wedding, and that he and his water-wife would live together happily for as long as they lived.

One day, Gwyn and his wife went to a funeral. Everyone round about had come to pay their last respects to the dead woman: she had been the daughter of a rich farmer and wife to the priest, generous with her time and money, and still in the prime of her life.

After the funeral, a good number of the priest's friends went back to his house to eat funeral cakes with him and keep him company, and Gwyn and his wife were among them.

No sooner had they stepped inside the priest's house than Gwyn's wife began to laugh. Amongst the mourners with their black suits and sober faces, she giggled as if she were tipsy with ale or romping with young children.

Gwyn was shocked. 'Shush!' he said. 'Think where you are! Stop this laughing!' he said. And firmly he laid a restraining hand on his wife's forearm.

'I'm laughing,' said Gwyn's wife, 'because when a person dies, she passes out of this world of trouble. Ah! Gwyn,' she cried, 'you've struck me for the third time and the last time. Our marriage is at an end.'

Gwyn's wife left the funeral feast alone and went straight back to their fine farm outside Myddfai. There she began to call in all her livestock.

'Brindled cow, come! White speckled cow, spotted cow, bold freckled cow, come! Old white-faced cow, Grey Squinter, white bull from the court of the king, come and come home!'

Gwyn's wife knew each of her livestock by name. And she did not forget the calf her husband had slaughtered only the previous week. 'Little black calf,' she cried, 'come down from the hook! Come home!'

The black calf leaped into life; it danced around the courtyard.

Then Gwyn's wife saw four of her oxen ploughing a nearby field. 'Grey oxen!' she cried. 'Four oxen of the field, you too must come home!'

When they heard her, the oxen turned from their task and, for all the whistles of the ploughboy, dragged the plough right across the newly turned furrows.

Gwyn's wife looked about her. She paused. Then she turned her back on the farmhouse and the farm. Those who saw her never forgot that sight: one woman, sad and steadfast, walking up on to Myddfai mountain, and behind her, plodding and trudging and tripping and high-stepping, a great concourse of creatures.

The woman crossed over on to the swept slopes of Black Mountain just above the lonely farm where Gwyn had been born and where Megan still lived in her old age. Up she climbed, on and up to the dark eye.

The Lady of Llyn y Fan Fach walked over the surface of the water and disappeared into the water, and all her hundreds of animals followed her. They left behind them sorrow, they left a wake of silence, and the deep furrow made by the oxen as they dragged their plough up over the shoulder of the mountain and into the lake.

One Night in Paradise

Once upon a time there were two close friends who, out of affection for each other, made this pledge: the first to get married would call on the other to be his best man, even if he should be at the ends of the earth.

Shortly thereafter one of the friends died. The survivor, who was planning to get married, had no idea what he should now do, so he sought the advice of his confessor.

'This is a ticklish situation,' said the priest, 'but you must keep your promise. Call on him even if he is dead. Go to his grave and say what you're supposed to say. It will then be up to him whether to come to your wedding or not.'

The youth went to the grave and said, 'Friend, the time has come for you to be my best man!'

The earth yawned, and out jumped the friend. 'By all means. I have to keep my word, or else I'd end up in Purgatory for no telling how long.'

They went home, and from there to church for the wedding. Then came the wedding banquet, where the dead youth told all kinds of stories, but not a word did he say about what he'd witnessed in the next world. The bridegroom longed to ask him some questions, but he didn't have the nerve. At the end of the banquet the dead man rose and said, 'Friend, since I've done you this favour, would you walk me back a part of the way?'

'Why, certainly! But I can't go far, naturally, since this is my wedding night.'

'I understand. You can turn back any time you like.'

The bridegroom kissed his bride. 'I'm going to step outside for a moment, and I'll be right back.' He walked out with the dead man. They chatted about first one thing and then another, and before you knew it, they were at the grave. There they embraced, and the living man thought, If I don't ask him now, I'll never ask him. He therefore took heart and said, 'Let me ask you something, since you are dead. What's it like in the hereafter?'

'I really can't say,' answered the dead man. 'If you want to find out, come along with me to Paradise.'

The grave opened, and the living man followed the dead one inside. Thus they found themselves in Paradise. The dead man took his friend to a handsome crystal palace with gold doors, where angels played their harps for blessed souls to dance, with Saint Peter strumming the double bass. The living man gaped at all the splendour, and goodness knows how long he would have remained in the palace if there hadn't been all the rest of Paradise to see.

'Come on to another spot now,' said the dead man, who led him into a garden whose trees, instead of foliage, displayed songbirds of every colour. 'Wake up, let's move on!' said the dead man, guiding his visitor on to a lawn where angels danced as joyously and gracefully as lovers. 'Next we'll go to see a star!' He could have gazed at the stars forever. Instead of water, their rivers ran with wine, and their land was of cheese.

All of a sudden, he started. 'Oh, my goodness, friend, it's later than I thought. I have to get back to my bride, who's surely worried about me.'

'Have you had enough of Paradise so soon?'

'Enough? If I had my choice . . .'

'And there's still so much to see.'

'I believe you, but I'd better be getting back.'

'Very well, suit yourself.' The dead man walked him back to the grave and vanished.

The living man stepped from the grave, but no longer recognized the cemetery. It was packed with monuments, statues, and tall trees. He left the cemetery and saw huge buildings in place of the simple stone cottages that used to line the streets. The streets were full of cars and buses, while aeroplanes flew through the skies.

'Where on earth am I? Did I take the wrong street? And look how these people are dressed!'

He stopped a little old man on the street. 'Sir, what is this town?'

'This city, you mean.'

'All right, this city. But I don't recognize it, for the life of me. Can you please direct me to the house of the man who got married yesterday?'

'Yesterday? I happen to be the sacristan, and I can assure you no one got married yesterday!'

'What do you mean? I got married myself!' Then he gave an account of accompanying his dead friend to Paradise.

'You're dreaming,' said the old man. 'That's an old story people tell about the bridegroom who followed his friend into the grave and never came back, while his bride died of sorrow.'

'That's not so, I'm the bridegroom myself!'

'Listen, the only thing for you to do is to go and speak with our bishop.'

'Bishop? But here in town there's only the parish priest.'

'What parish priest? For years and years we've had a bishop.' And the sacristan took him to the bishop.

The youth told his story to the bishop, who recalled an event he'd heard about as a boy. He took down the parish books and began flipping back the pages. Thirty years ago, no. Fifty years ago, no. One hundred, no. Two hundred, no. He went on thumbing the pages. Finally on a yellowed, crumbling page he put his finger on those very names. 'It was three hundred years ago. The young man disappeared from the cemetery, and the bride died of a broken heart. Read right here if you don't believe it!'

'But I'm the bridegroom myself!'

'And you went to the next world? Tell me about it!'

But the young man turned deathly pale, sank to the ground, and died before he could tell one single thing he had seen.

Oniyeye and King Olu Dotun's Daughter

A very long time ago, and soon after our forefathers had come to Yorubaland, there lived a king called Olu Dotun. This king had only one child, a very beautiful daughter, and when she reached a marriageable age, her father was unable to decide to whom she should be married. Many young men had asked for the girl as wife, but the king had refused them all. In order to rid himself of the many suitors that called at his palace, he announced one day, half in jest, that any man in the kingdom who was able to produce an animal with one hundred and fifty-two tails could have half the kingdom and the hand of his daughter in marriage.

The king's news was received with great surprise by all the hunters. One of them, called Oniyeye, who was reputed to be the finest of them all in the king's dominion, made up his mind that if such an animal existed in the world, he would hunt it down and bring it to the king.

First he went and called on an Ifa priest and asked him to find out if there really was such an animal in the world. The priest, for a small gift, promised to consult his jujus and let him know. Three days later the Ifa priest called him back. 'Yes,' said the old man, 'such an animal does exist today, but only one remains in the whole world. My juju tells me that it dwells in a far-distant hollow mountain, but where it is I do not know. Nobody can reach it except in their dreams, and if you do ever happen to dream of the animal you must make a sacrifice to the gods on waking. Beyond this I can tell you nothing more, my son.'

Oniyeye thanked the old Ifa priest and departed.

For a long time the hunter tried to find out how he could reach the hollow mountain where the animal with a hundred and fifty-two tails dwelt. At last he thought of a plan.

He told all his friends and brother hunters that he was going away on a long journey and would not be returning for two months, and so he set out with his bow and arrows, and armed with his hunter's talisman.

Setting off for the forest on foot, he travelled for several days, until he came to a district where many of the wild animals congregated.

Oniyeye searched about until he discovered an open glade. This showed signs of being frequented by many animals. He then placed his quivers under his head as a pillow and his bow under his feet and lay still, pretending to be dead.

For a long time Oniyeye lay perfectly still. Gradually, however, being on the ground and being a skilled hunter, he was able to discern movements in the undergrowth of the forest, sounds that were not made by the wind. Suddenly a tiny field-mouse appeared and watched Oniyeye for a long time from a little distance, then, growing bolder, he came up close to the hunter and looked again. All this while Oniyeye kept his eyes closed and pretended to be dead.

Now the field-mouse had often been warned about Oniyeye and of his great skill as a hunter. He was well known to the creatures of the forest, who were quick to inform each other if he was hunting in the district. They always knew Oniyeye by his talisman.

The field-mouse started to sing and call all the other animals to come and witness that the greatest of all hunters, Oniyeye, was dead and peace and safety had once more returned to the forest. He was soon heard by the monkeys, and their loud chattering attracted other animals. So one by one all the animals from the district gathered in the glade till it was full and there was great rejoicing amongst them. Not only the animals, but the birds and insects too gathered to celebrate the good news. Returning to their homes, they called on all their companions to go and look at the corpse of Oniyeye lying in the glade and spread the report that he was now dead.

The animal with one hundred and fifty-two tails learnt the news from some birds that happened to be flying home across the hollow mountain, chirping with joy. He called one of the birds and asked him if the news was correct. 'Go and see for yourself,' replied the bird. 'You will see all the other animals around the hunter's body in the glade.'

'Good, go back and announce to the animals that I, the animal of one hundred and fifty-two tails, am coming to witness Oniyeye's death, and tell them to prepare for my coming.'

The bird flew back and informed the others, and so the hunter knew that his plan had worked.

Coming down from his hollow mountain, the animal with one hundred and fifty-two tails went to the glade. When he appeared, all the other animals were impressed and prostrating themselves on the ground, hailed him as their king.

'This is a great day for all of us,' said the king of the animals. 'This man Oniyeye was the most powerful hunter in the world and because of him, my friends, I have shut myself up alone in the hollow mountain for many years. Now that I have witnessed his death I will come down, and henceforth I will live here in the forest amongst you all.' There was a roar of applause at these words, and the animals took their king to see the hunter's body.

Then the king started to boast of his great power. 'Now pick up the dead Oniyeye,' ordered the animal of one hundred and fifty-two tails, 'and carry him back to my hollow mountain while I mount him like a horse and ride home in triumph.'

At these words, Oniyeye sprang up, seizing his bow and arrows as he did so. There was a great cry of astonishment and fear from everybody, and instead of staying to help their king, the animals fled in confusion into the forest. As for the animal with one hundred and fifty-two tails, he lay there quivering before the hunter.

Oniyeye was about to kill the animal, but he begged the hunter to spare his life and said he would become his slave and work for him for the rest of his life.

So Oniyeye spared him and carried him back to King Olu Dotun.

There was great excitement and rejoicing when they reached the king's palace, and people came from far and wide to witness the strange animal with so many tails.

As for the other hunters, some had been able to find animals with as many as fifty tails and one hunter had even found one with one hundred tails. King Olu Dotun had, however, particularly announced that he would give his daughter in marriage to the man who produced one with one hundred and fifty-two. So Oniyeye married the king's daughter and was given half the kingdom to rule over. As for the animal of one hundred and fifty-two tails, he lived peacefully in captivity, and the other animals of the forest enjoyed greater security, for Oniyeye did not go hunting so often after his marriage.

Why the Hare Runs Away

This is a story of the hare and the other animals.

The dry weather was drying up the earth into hardness. There was no dew. Even the creatures of the water suffered from thirst. Famine soon followed, and the animals, having nothing to eat, assembled in council.

'What shall we do,' said they, 'to keep ourselves from dying of hunger and thirst?' And they deliberated a long time.

At last it was decided that each animal should cut off the tips of its ears, and extract the fat from them. Then all the fat would be collected and sold, and with the money they would get for it, they would buy a hoe and dig a well, so as to get some water.

And all cried, 'It is well. Let us cut off the tips of our ears.'

They did so, but when it came the hare's turn he refused.

The other animals were astonished, but they said nothing. They took up the ears, extracted the fat, went and sold all, and bought a hoe with the money.

They brought back the hoe and began to dig a well in the dry bed of a lagoon, until at last they found water. They said, 'Ha! At last we can slake our thirst a little.'

The hare was not there, but when the sun was in the middle of the sky, he took a calabash and went towards the well.

As he walked along, the calabash dragged on the ground and made a great noise. It said, '*Chan-gan-gan-gan, chan-gan-gan-gan.*'

The animals, who were watching by the lagoon, heard this terrible noise and were frightened.

They asked each other, 'What is it?' Then, as the noise kept coming nearer, they ran away. Reaching home, they said something terrible at the lagoon had put them to flight.

When all the animals were gone, the hare could draw up water from the lagoon without interference. Then he went down into the well and bathed, so that the water was muddied.

When the next day came, all the animals ran to get water, and they found it muddied.

'Oh,' they cried, 'who has spoiled our well?'

Saying this, they went and took a dummy-image. They made birdlime and spread it over the image.

Then, when the sun was again in the middle of the sky, all the animals went and hid in the bush near the well.

Soon the hare came, his calabash crying, '*Chan-gan-gan-gan, chan-gan-gan-gan.*' He approached the image. He never suspected that all the animals were hidden in the bush.

The hare saluted the image. The image said nothing. He saluted again, and still the image said nothing.

'Take care,' said the hare, 'or I will give you a slap.'

He gave it a slap, and his right hand was stuck fast in the birdlime. He slapped with his left hand, and that was held fast, too.

'Oh! oh!' cried he, 'I'll kick with my feet,' and he did, but his feet became fixed, and he could not get away.

Then the animals ran out of the bush and came to see the hare and his calabash.

'Shame, shame, oh, hare!' they cried together. 'Did you not agree with us to cut off the tips of your ears, and, when it came to your turn, did you not refuse? What! You refused, and yet you come to muddy our water?'

They took whips, they fell upon the hare, and they beat him. They beat him so that they nearly killed him.

'We ought to kill you, accursed hare,' they said. 'But no—run.'

They let him go, and the hare fled. Since then, he does not leave the grass.

The Sacred Milk of Koumongoé

Far away, in a very hot country, there once lived a man and woman who had two children, a son named Koané and a daughter called Thakané.

Early in the morning and late in the evenings the parents worked hard in the fields, resting, when the sun was high, under the shade of some tree. While they were absent the little girl kept house alone, for her brother always got up before the dawn, when the air was fresh and cool, and drove out the cattle to the sweetest patches of grass he could find.

One day, when Koané had slept later than usual, his father and mother went to their work before him, and there was only Thakané to be seen busy making the bread for supper.

'Thakané,' he said, 'I am thirsty. Give me a drink from the tree Koumongoé, which has the best milk in the world.'

'Oh, Koané,' cried his sister, 'you know that we are forbidden to touch that tree. What would father say when he came home? For he would be sure to know.'

'Nonsense,' replied Koané, 'there is so much milk in Koumongoé that he will never miss a little. If you won't give it to me, I shan't take the cattle out. They will just have to stay all day in the hut, and you know that they will starve.'

And he turned from her in a rage, and sat down in the corner.

After a while Thakané said to him: 'It is getting hot, had you not better drive out the cattle now?'

But Koané only answered sulkily, 'I told you I am not going to drive them out at all. If I have to do without milk, they shall do without grass.'

Thakané did not know what to do. She was afraid to disobey her parents, who would most likely beat her, yet the beasts would be sure to suffer if they were kept in, and she would perhaps be beaten for that too. So at last she took an axe and a tiny earthen bowl, she cut a very small hole in the side of Koumongoé, and out gushed enough milk to fill the bowl.

'Here is the milk you wanted,' said she, going up to Koané, who was still sulking in his corner.

'What is the use of that?' grumbled Koané. 'Why, there is not enough to drown a fly. Go and get me three times as much!'

Trembling with fright, Thakané returned to the tree, and struck it a sharp blow with the axe. In an instant there poured forth such a stream of milk that it ran like a river into the hut.

'Koané! Koané!' cried she. 'Come and help me to plug up the hole. There will be no milk left for our father and mother.' But Koané could not stop it any more than Thakané, and soon the milk was flowing through the hut downhill towards their parents in the fields below.

The man saw the white stream a long way off, and guessed what had happened.

'Wife, wife,' he called loudly to the woman, who was working at a little distance, 'do you see Koumongoé running fast down the hill? That is some mischief of the children's, I am sure. I must go home and find out what is the matter.' And they both threw down their hoes and hurried to the side of Koumongoé.

Kneeling on the grass, the man and his wife made a cup of their hands and drank the milk from it. And no sooner had they done this than Koumongoé flowed back again up the hill, and entered the hut.

'Thakané,' said the parents, severely, when they reached home panting from the heat of the sun, 'what have you been doing? Why did Koumongoé come to us in the fields instead of staying in the garden?'

'It was Koané's fault,' answered Thakané. 'He would not take the cattle to feed until he drank some of the milk from Koumongoé. So, as I did not know what else to do, I gave it to him.'

The father listened to Thakané's words, but made no answer. Instead, he went outside and brought in two sheepskins which he stained red, and sent for a blacksmith to forge some iron rings. The rings were then passed over Thakané's arms and legs and neck, and the skins fastened on her before and behind. When all was ready, the man sent for his servants and said, 'I am going to get rid of Thakané.'

'Get rid of your only daughter?' they answered, in surprise. 'But why?'

'Because she has eaten what she ought not to have eaten. She has touched the sacred tree which belongs to her mother and me alone.' And, turning his back, he called to Thakané to follow him, and they went down the road which led to the dwelling of an ogre.

They were passing along some fields where the corn was ripening, when a rabbit suddenly sprang out at their feet, and standing on its hind legs, it sang:

Why do you give to the ogre
Your child, so fair, so fair?

'You had better ask her,' replied the man, 'she is old enough to give you an answer.'

Then, in her turn, Thakané sang:

I gave Koumongoé to Koané,
Koumongoé to the keeper of beasts;
For without Koumongoé they could not go to the meadows:
Without Koumongoé they would starve in the hut;
That was why I gave him the Koumongoé of my father.

And when the rabbit heard that, he cried, 'Wretched man! It is you whom the ogre should eat, and not your beautiful daughter.'

But the father paid no heed to what the rabbit said, and only walked on the faster, bidding Thakané to keep close behind him. By-and-by they met with a troop of great deer, called elands, and they stopped when they saw Thakané and sang:

Why do you give to the ogre
Your child, so fair, so fair?

'You had better ask her,' replied the man, 'she is old enough to give you an answer.'

Then, in her turn, Thakané sang:

I gave Koumongoé to Koané,
Koumongoé to the keeper of beasts;
For without Koumongoé they could not go to the meadows:
Without Koumongoé they would starve in the hut;
That was why I gave him the Koumongoé of my father.

And the elands all cried, 'Wretched man! It is you whom the ogre should eat, and not your beautiful daughter.'

By this time it was nearly dark, and the father said they could travel no further that night, and must go to sleep where they were. Thakané was thankful indeed when she heard this, for she was very tired, and found the two skins fastened round her almost too heavy to carry. So, in spite of her dread of the ogre, she slept till dawn, when her father woke her, and told her roughly that he was ready to continue their journey.

Crossing the plain, the girl and her father passed a herd of gazelles feeding. They lifted their heads, wondering who was out so early, and when they caught sight of Thakané, they sang:

Why do you give to the ogre
Your child, so fair, so fair?

'You had better ask her,' replied the man, 'she is old enough to answer for herself.'

Then, in her turn, Thakané sang:

I gave Koumongoé to Koané,
Koumongoé to the keeper of beasts;

For without Koumongoé they could not go to the meadows:
Without Koumongoé they would starve in the hut;
That was why I gave him the Koumongoé of my father.

And the gazelles all cried, 'Wretched man! It is you whom the ogre should eat, and not your beautiful daughter.'

At last they arrived at the village where the ogre lived, and they went straight to his hut. He was nowhere to be seen, but in his place was his son Masilo, who was not an ogre at all, but a very polite young man. He ordered his servants to bring a pile of skins for Thakané to sit on, but told her father he must sit on the ground. Then, catching sight of the girl's face, which she had kept bent down, he was struck by its beauty, and put the same question that the rabbit, and the elands, and the gazelles had done.

Thakané answered him as before, and he instantly commanded that she should be taken to the hut of his mother, and placed under her care, while the man should be led to his father. Directly the ogre saw him he bade the servant throw him into the great pot which always stood ready on the fire, and in five minutes he was done to a turn. After that the servant returned to Masilo and related all that had happened.

Now Masilo had fallen in love with Thakané the moment he saw her. At first he did not know what to make of this strange feeling, for all his life he had hated women, and had refused several brides whom his parents had chosen for him. However, they were so anxious that he should marry, that they willingly accepted Thakané as their daughter-in-law, though she did not bring any marriage portion with her.

After some time a baby was born to her, and Thakané thought it was the most beautiful baby that ever was seen. But when her mother-in-law saw it was a girl, she wrung her hands and wept, saying, 'O miserable mother! Miserable child! Alas for you! Why were you not a boy!'

Thakané, in great surprise, asked the meaning of her distress; and the old woman told her that it was the custom in that country that all the girls who were born should be given to the ogre to eat.

Then Thakané clasped the baby tightly in her arms, and cried, 'But it is not the custom in my country! There, when children die, they are buried in the earth. No one shall take my baby from me.'

That night, when everyone in the hut was asleep, Thakané rose, and carrying her baby on her back, went down to a place where the river spread itself out into a large lake, with tall willows all round the bank. Here, hidden from everyone, she sat down on a stone and began to think what she should do to save her child.

Suddenly she heard a rustling among the willows, and an old woman appeared before her.

'What are you crying for, my dear?' said she.

And Thakané answered, 'I was crying for my baby—I cannot hide her for ever, and if the ogre sees her, he will eat her; and I would rather she was drowned than that.'

'What you say is true,' replied the old woman. 'Give me your child, and let me take care of it. And if you will fix a day to meet me here I will bring the baby.'

Then Thakané dried her eyes, and gladly accepted the old woman's offer. When she got home she told her husband she had thrown it in the river, and as he had watched her go in that direction he never thought of doubting what she said.

On the appointed day, Thakané slipped out when everybody was busy, and ran down the path that led to the lake. As soon as she got there, she crouched down among the willows, and sang softly:

Bring to me Dilah, Dilah the rejected one,
Dilah, whom her father Masilo cast out!

And in a moment the old woman appeared holding the baby in her arms. Dilah had become so big and strong, that Thakané's heart was filled with joy and gratitude, and she stayed as long as she dared, playing with her baby.

At last she felt she must return to the village, lest she should be missed, and the child was handed back to the old woman, who vanished with her into the lake.

Children grow up very quickly when they live under water, and in less time than anyone could suppose, Dilah had changed from a baby to a woman. Her mother came to visit her whenever she was able, and one day, when they were sitting talking together, they were spied by a man who had come to cut willows to weave into baskets. He was so surprised to see how like the face of the girl was to Masilo, that he left his work and returned to the village.

'Masilo,' he said, as he entered the hut, 'I have just beheld your wife near the river with a girl who must be your daughter, she is so like you. We have been deceived, for we all thought she was dead.'

When he heard this, Masilo tried to look shocked because his wife had broken the law; but in his heart he was very glad.

'But what shall we do now?' asked he.

'Make sure for yourself that I am speaking the truth by hiding among the bushes the first time Thakané says she is going to bathe in the river, and waiting till the girl appears.'

For some days Thakané stayed quietly at home, and her husband began to think that the man had been mistaken; but at last she said to her husband: 'I am going to bathe in the river.'

'Well, you can go,' answered he. But he ran down quickly by another path, and got there first, and hid himself in the bushes.

An instant later, Thakané arrived, and standing on the bank, she sang:

Bring to me Dilah, Dilah the rejected one,
Dilah, whom her father Masilo cast out!

Then the old woman came out of the water, holding the girl, now tall and slender, by the hand. And as Masilo looked, he saw that she was indeed his daughter, and he wept for joy that she was not lying dead in the bottom of the lake.

The old woman, however, seemed uneasy, and said to Thakané, 'I feel as if someone was watching us. I will not leave the girl today, but will take her back with me.' And sinking beneath the surface, she drew the girl after her. After they had gone, Thakané returned to the village, which Masilo had managed to reach before her.

All the rest of the day Masilo sat in a corner weeping, and his mother who came in asked, 'Why are you weeping so bitterly, my son?'

'My head aches,' he answered, 'it aches very badly.' And his mother passed on, and left him alone.

In the evening he said to his wife, 'I have seen my daughter, in the place where you told me you had drowned her. Instead, she lives at the bottom of the lake, and has now grown into a young woman.'

'I don't know what you are talking about,' replied Thakané. 'I buried my child under the sand on the beach.'

Then Masilo implored her to give the child back to him; but she would not listen, and only answered, 'If I were to give her back you would only obey the laws of your country and take her to your father, the ogre, and she would be eaten.'

But Masilo promised that he would never let his father see her, and that now she was a woman no one would try to hurt her; so Thakané's heart melted, and she went down to the lake to consult the old woman.

'What am I to do?' she asked, when, after clapping her hands, the old woman appeared before her. 'Yesterday Masilo beheld Dilah, and ever since he has entreated me to give him back his daughter.'

'If I let her go he must pay me a thousand head of cattle in exchange,' replied the old woman. And Thakané carried her answer back to Masilo.

'Why, I would gladly give her two thousand!' cried he, 'for she has saved my daughter.' And he bade messengers hasten to all the neighbouring villages, and tell his people to send him at once all the cattle he possessed. When they were all assembled he chose a thousand of the finest bulls and cows, and drove them down to the river, followed by a great crowd wondering what would happen.

Then Thakané stepped forward in front of the cattle and sang:

Bring to me Dilah, Dilah the rejected one,
Dilah, whom her father Masilo cast out!

And Dilah came from the waters holding out her hands to Masilo and Thakané, and in her place the cattle sank into the lake, and were driven by the old woman to the great city filled with people, which lies at the bottom.

The Magic Mirror

A long, long while ago, before ever the White Men were seen in Senna, there lived a man called Gopáni-Kúfa.

One day, as he was out hunting, he came upon a strange sight. An enormous python had caught an antelope and coiled itself around it; the antelope, striking out in despair with its horns, had pinned the python's neck to a tree, and so deeply had its horns sunk in the soft wood that neither creature could get away.

'Help!' cried the antelope. 'For I was doing no harm, yet I have been caught, and would have been eaten, had I not defended myself.'

'Help me,' said the python, 'for I am Insáto, King of all the Reptiles, and will reward you well!'

Gopáni-Kúfa considered for a moment, then stabbing the antelope with his assegai, he set the python free.

'I thank you,' said the python. 'Come back here with the new moon, when I shall have eaten the antelope, and I will reward you as I promised.'

'Yes,' said the dying antelope, 'he will reward you and lo! your reward shall be your own undoing!'

Gopáni-Kúfa went back to his kraal, and with the new moon he returned again to the spot where he had saved the python.

Insáto was lying upon the ground, still sleepy from the effects of his huge meal, and when he saw the man he thanked him again, and said, 'Come with me now to Píta, which is my own country, and I will give you what you will of all my possessions.'

Gopáni-Kúfa at first was afraid, thinking of what the antelope had said, but finally he consented and followed Insáto into the forest.

For several days they travelled, and at last they came to a hole leading deep into the earth. It was not very wide, but large enough to admit a man. 'Hold on to my tail,' said Insáto, 'and I will go down first, drawing you after me.' The man did so, and Insáto entered.

Down, down, down they went for days, all the while getting deeper and deeper into the earth, until at last the darkness ended and they dropped into a beautiful country; around them grew short green grass, on which browsed herds of cattle and sheep and goats. In the distance Gopáni-Kúfa saw a great collection of houses all square, built of stone and very tall, and their roofs were shining with gold and burnished iron.

Gopáni-Kúfa turned to Insáto, but found, in the place of the python, a man, strong and handsome, with the great snake's skin wrapped round him for covering; and on his arms and neck were rings of pure gold.

The man smiled. 'I am Insáto,' said he, 'but in my own country I take man's shape—even as you see me—for this is Píta, the land over which I am king.' He then took Gopáni-Kúfa by the hand and led him towards the town.

On the way they passed rivers in which men and women were bathing and fishing and boating; and further on they came to gardens covered with heavy crops of rice and maize, and many other grains which Gopáni-Kúfa did not even know the name of. And as they passed, the people who were singing at their work in the fields abandoned their labours and saluted Insáto with delight, bringing also palm wine and green coconuts for refreshment, as to one returned from a long journey.

'These are my children!' said Insáto, waving his hand towards the people. Gopáni-Kúfa was much astonished at all that he saw, but he said nothing. Presently they came to the town; everything here, too, was beautiful, and everything that a man might desire he could obtain. Even the grains of dust in the streets were of gold and silver.

Insáto conducted Gopáni-Kúfa to the palace, and showing him his rooms, and the maidens who would wait upon him, told him that they would have a great feast that night, and on the morrow he might name his choice of the riches of Píta and it should be given him. Then he went away.

Now Gopáni-Kúfa had a wasp called Zéngi-mízi. Zéngi-mízi was not an ordinary wasp, for the spirit of the father of Gopáni-Kúfa had entered it, so that it was exceedingly wise. In times of doubt Gopáni-Kúfa always consulted the wasp as to what had better be done, so on this occasion he took it out of the little rush basket in which he carried it, saying, 'Zéngi-mízi, what gift shall I ask of Insáto tomorrow when he would know the reward he shall bestow on me for saving his life?'

'Biz-z-z,' hummed Zéngi-mízi, 'ask him for Sipáo the Mirror.' And it flew back into its basket.

Gopáni-Kúfa was astonished at this answer; but knowing that the words of Zéngi-mízi were true words, he determined to make the request. So that night they feasted, and on the morrow Insáto came to Gopáni-Kúfa and, giving him greeting joyfully, he said, 'Now, O my friend, name your choice amongst my possessions and you shall have it!'

'O king!' answered Gopáni-Kúfa, 'out of all your possessions I will have the Mirror, Sipáo.'

The king started. 'O friend, Gopáni-Kúfa,' he said, 'ask anything but that! I did not think that you would request that which is most precious to me.'

'Let me think over it again then, O king,' said Gopáni-Kúfa, 'and tomorrow I will let you know if I change my mind.'

But the king was still much troubled, fearing the loss of Sipáo, for the Mirror had magic powers, so that he who owned it had but to ask and his wish would be fulfilled; to it Insáto owed all that he possessed.

As soon as the king left him, Gopáni-Kúfa again took Zéngi-mízi out of his basket. 'Zéngi-mízi,' he said, 'the king seems loath to grant my request for the Mirror—is there not some other thing of equal value for which I might ask?'

And the wasp answered, 'There is nothing in the world, O Gopáni-Kúfa, which is of such value as this Mirror, for it is a Wishing Mirror, and accomplishes the desires of him who owns it. If the king hesitates, go to him the next day, and the day after, and in the end he will bestow the Mirror upon you, for you saved his life.'

And it was even so. For three days Gopáni-Kúfa returned the same answer to the king, and, at last, with tears in his eyes, Insáto gave him the Mirror, which was of polished iron, saying, 'Take Sipáo, then, O Gopáni-Kúfa, and may thy wishes come true. Go back now to thine own country; Sipáo will show you the way.'

Gopáni-Kúfa was greatly rejoiced, and, taking farewell of the king, said to the Mirror, 'Sipáo, Sipáo, I wish to be back upon the Earth again!'

Instantly he found himself standing upon the upper earth; but, not knowing the spot, he said again to the Mirror, 'Sipáo, Sipáo, I want the path to my own kraal!'

And behold! right before him lay the path!

When he arrived home he found his wife and daughter mourning for him, for they thought that he had been eaten by lions; but he comforted them, saying that while following a wounded antelope he had missed his way and had wandered for a long time before he had found the path again.

That night he asked Zéngi-mízi, in whom sat the spirit of his father, what he had better ask Sipáo for next?

'Biz-z-z,' said the wasp, 'would you not like to be as great a chief as Insáto?'

And Gopáni-Kúfa smiled, and took the Mirror and said to it, 'Sipáo, Sipáo, I want a town as great as that of Insáto, the King of Píta; and I wish to be chief over it!'

Then all along the banks of the Zambesi river, which flowed near by, sprang up streets of stone buildings, and their roofs shone with gold and burnished iron like those in Píta; and in the streets men and women were walking, and young boys were driving out the sheep and cattle to pasture; and from the river came shouts and laughter from the young men and maidens who had launched their canoes and were fishing. And when the people of the new town beheld Gopáni-Kúfa they rejoiced greatly and hailed him as chief.

Gopáni-Kúfa was now as powerful as Insáto the King of the Reptiles had been, and he and his family moved into the palace that stood high above the other buildings right in the middle of the town. His wife was too astonished at all these wonders to ask any questions, but his daughter Shasása kept begging him to tell her how he had suddenly become so great; so at last he revealed the whole secret, and even entrusted Sipáo the Mirror to her care, saying, 'It will be safer with you, my daughter, for you dwell apart; whereas men come to consult me on affairs of state, and the Mirror might be stolen.'

Then Shasása took the Magic Mirror and hid it beneath her pillow, and after that for many years Gopáni-Kúfa ruled his people both well and wisely, so that all men loved him, and never once did he need to ask Sipáo to grant him a wish.

Now it happened that, after many years, when the hair of Gopáni-Kúfa was turning grey with age, there came white men to that country. Up the Zambesi they came, and they fought long and fiercely with Gopáni-Kúfa; but, because of the power of the Magic Mirror, he beat them, and they fled to the sea-coast. Chief among them was one Rei, a man of much cunning, who sought to discover whence sprang Gopáni-Kúfa's power. So one day he called to him a trusty servant named Butou, and said, 'Go you to the town and find out for me what is the secret of its greatness.'

And Butou, dressing himself in rags, set out, and when he came to Gopáni-Kúfa's town he asked for the chief; and the people took him into the presence of Gopáni-Kúfa. When the white man saw him he humbled himself, and said, 'O Chief! take pity on me, for I have no home! When Rei marched against you I alone stood apart, for I knew that all the strength of the Zambesi lay in your hands, and because I would not fight against you he turned me forth into the forest to starve!'

And Gopáni-Kúfa believed the white man's story, and he took him in and feasted him, and gave him a house.

In this way the end came. For the heart of Shasása, the daughter of Gopáni-Kúfa, went forth to Butou the traitor, and from her he learnt the secret of the Magic Mirror. One night, when all the town slept, he felt beneath her pillow and, finding the Mirror, he stole it and fled back with it to Rei, the chief of the white men.

So it befell that, one day, as Gopáni-Kúfa was gazing at the river from a window of the palace he again saw the war-canoes of the white men; and at the sight his spirit misgave him.

'Shasása! My daughter!' he cried wildly. 'Go fetch me the Mirror, for the white men are at hand.'

'Woe is me, my father!' she sobbed. 'The Mirror is gone! For I loved Butou the traitor, and he has stolen Sipáo from me!'

Then Gopáni-Kúfa calmed himself, and drew out Zéngi-mízi from its rush basket.

'O spirit of my father!' he said. 'What now shall I do?'

'O Gopáni-Kúfa!' hummed the wasp. 'There is nothing now that can be done, for the words of the antelope which you slew are being fulfilled.'

'Alas! I am an old man—I had forgotten!' cried the chief. 'The words of the antelope were true words—my reward shall be my own undoing—they are being fulfilled!'

Then the white men fell upon the people of Gopáni-Kúfa and slew them together with the chief and his daughter Shasása; and since then all the power of the Earth has rested in the hands of the white men, for they have in their possession Sipáo, the Magic Mirror.

Glossary

dervish: a man of Muslim faith who has taken vows of poverty

dreidel: a Jewish four-sided spinning-top; the game played with it

fakir: a man of Hindu or Muslim faith sworn to poverty

ghoul: evil spirit who robs graves and eats corpses

gourd: large fruit used as vessel when dried and hollowed out

hamal: porter

Hanukkah: 8-day midwinter Jewish festival commemorating the rededication of the Temple. Also known as the Festival of Lights

jinn (or djinn): supernatural beings in Muslim legend that can take human or animal form, and influence human affairs

juju: a magic charm used by some West African tribes; or the magic the charm works

kismet: fate

kvass: a Russian fermented drink made from barley or rye

muezzin: public crier who proclaims the hours of prayer from the slender tower of a mosque, known as a minaret

sesame: kind of seed, yielding oil

scree: steep slope of stones on a mountainside

tabor: small drum

Acknowledgements

Roger D. Abrahams: 'Why the Hare Runs Away' from *African Folktales,* Copyright © 1983 by Roger D. Abrahams, reprinted by permission of Pantheon Books, a division of Random House, Inc. **Inea Bushnaq:** 'The Nightingale that Shrieked' from *Arab Folktales* edited and translated by Inea Bushnaq, Copyright © 1986 by Inea Bushnaq, reprinted by permission of Pantheon Books, a division of Random House, Inc. **Italo Calvino:** 'One Night in Paradise' from *Italian Folktales:* Selected and retold by Italo Calvino (1980), Copyright © 1956 by Giulio Einaudi Editore, s.p.a., English translation by George Martin, Copyright © 1980 by Harcourt Inc., reprinted by permission of Harcourt Inc. **Kevin Crossley-Holland:** 'The Pied Piper of Hamelin' first published in *Tales from Europe* (BBC Books, 1991), reprinted by permission of the author c/o Rogers, Colridge & White Ltd, 20 Powis Mews, London W11 1JN; 'The Three Blows', from *Enchantment: Fairy Tales, Ghost Stories and Tales of Wonder* (Orion Children's Books 2000), reprinted by permission of The Orion Publishing Group Ltd. **Charles Downing:** 'The Power of Love' from *Armenian Folk-tales and Fables* (OUP, 1972). **Abayomi Fuja:** 'Oniyeye and King Olu Dotun's Daughter' from *Fourteen Hundred Cowries* (OUP, Ibadan, 1962). **A. K. Ramanujan:** 'And then, *Burrah!*' from *Folktales from India*, Copyright © 1991 by A. K. Ramanujan, reprinted by permission of Pantheon Books, a division of Random House, Inc. **Jacqueline Simpson:** 'The Dead Man's Nightcap' from *Icelandic Folktales and Legends* (1972). **Isaac Bashevis Singer:** 'Zlateh the Goat' from *Zlateh the Goat and other Stories* (Harper & Row, 1966), text copyright © 1966 by Isaac Bashevis Singer, reprinted by permission of HarperCollins Publishers, Inc. **Barbara K. Walker:** 'Trousers Mehmet and the Sultan's Daughter'; from *A Treasury of Turkish Folktales for Children*, Copyright © 1988 by Barbara K. Walker, reprinted by permission of Linnet Books/The Shoe String Press, Inc., North Haven, Connecticut, USA.

Although we have tried to trace and contact all copyright holders before publication this has not been possible in every case. If notified we will rectify any errors or omissions at the earliest opportunity.

We also acknowledge with thanks the following out-of-copyright material: **C. Fillingham-Coxwell:** 'Vasilissa the Fair' from *Siberian and Other Folktales* (London, 1925). **Andrew Lang:** 'The Forty Thieves' from *The Blue Fairy Book*; 'Stan Bolovan' from *The Violet Fairy Book*; 'The Sacred Milk of Koumongoe' from *The Brown Fairy Book*; 'The Magic Mirror' from *The Orange Fairy Book*.

The editor is grateful to Margaret Lockerbie Cameron, Keith Harrison, Ron Heapy, David Lumsdaine, Eric Maddern, Linda Waslien, and Gillian Crossley-Holland for their valuable advice and pursuit of elusive tales.

And Then, Bhurrah!

A storyteller was tired of telling stories, but the children and the grown people who were around him were not yet tired of listening to them. They asked for more.

So he began to describe how a vast number of birds were sitting on a tree. People asked as usual at a pause, 'And then?'

He said, 'One bird flew from the tree with a sound like *bhurrah!*'

'And then?'

'*Bhurrah!* went another bird, flying from the tree.'

'And then?'

'Another bird went *bhurrah!*'

'And then?'

'*Bhurrah!*'

This went on until nothing was heard but 'And then?' and '*Bhurrah!*' Finally someone asked, 'How long is this going to go on?' The storyteller answered, 'Till all the birds are gone.'

OTHER BOOKS BY KEVIN CROSSLEY-HOLLAND

Why the Fish Laughed and Other Tales

0 19 275187 5

Carnegie medal winner Kevin Crossley-Holland has made a sparkling selection of stories from Asia and India, the Americas and the Pacific. Together they celebrate the many different customs and approaches to life around the world.

A laughing fish? Everything is possible in these magical tales from around the world. You'll meet rainbow birds, cackling witches, and tiger-tamers in this lively and surprising collection.

Why the Fish Laughed is a companion volume to *The Nightingale that Shrieked*, also published by Oxford.

Short! A Book of Very Short Stories

0 19 278148 0

This is a book of the shortest stories—some familiar, some brand new, and some retold in a different way. There are ghost stories and wonder tales, fables, practical jokes, modern horror stories, and myths. The stories include Anansi the spider man, the ghost on the bridge, people who make the right or wrong choice, animals that talk (of course), and a little voice in a dark room (when there shouldn't be anyone there).

Many, many stories. That's enough. Best to keep it short!

Tales from West Africa

Martin Bennett

ISBN 0 19 275076 3

This lively collection comes from West Africa, a place 'where stories grow on trees'. Here are the famous tricksters: Hare, Tortoise, and the greatest of them all – Ananse the spider. The stories are full of larger-than-life characters and situations; and include the tale of how Ananse got his thin waist, how Crocodile learnt his lesson, and how Monkey managed not to get eaten by Shark.

Tales from China

Cyril Birch

ISBN 0 19 275078 X

This collection of Chinese stories begins with the great legends of how Earth and Heaven came into being, and of how the archer Yi rid the Emperor Yao of the menace of the ten suns. There are folk-tales too, about ghosts and rain-makers, poor students and magicians, and the man who was nearly made into fishpaste. Throughout all these stories the author has kept the subtle oriental flavour of the originals and brings to life all the magic and mystery of China.

Fairy Tales from England

James Reeves

ISBN 0 19 275014 3

Giant-killing Johnny Gloke, a princess with a sheep's head, and a frog prince at the World's End are just some of the fairy-tale characters you'll find in this collection of stories, along with better-known tales such as Dick Whittington and Tom Thumb. Greedy giants, handsome princes, wicked queens, and a liberal sprinkling of magic all help to make sure this collection of traditional English fairy-tales has something for everyone.

Fairy Tales from Scotland

Barbara Ker Wilson

ISBN 0 19 275012 7

Gallant knights, the enchanting Elf Queen, witches, wizards, and wee faery folk . . . you'll find them all in this exciting collection of Scottish fairy tales and legends. Whether you prefer Highland legends, ancient sagas, or warrior adventures, there's something for everyone in this collection – along with a good helping of Gaelic magic!